FAIRHOPE OPHELIA

FAIRHOPE OPHELIA

ACKNOWLEDGEMENT

Thank you to Fairhope for an extraordinary place to write my book series. I've been toting my laptop in and out of the bars, bistros, coffee shops and restaurants for the last year and a half enjoying the writing process while dining on delicious food and drinks.

I would like to dedicate this book to my family and friends.

I appreciate your encouraging words and love.

~~Ansley

CONTENTS

CHAPTER 1

Ophelia Griffin opened the front door to the Bone and Barrel Restaurant and Bar. It looked the same as it had three years ago with the exception of new barstools and a few new pieces of artwork hanging on the walls. The bar rail was to the left with tables for dining to the right. There was a small stage pushed back in the right corner for a one-man band, but it was empty. Instead music was being pumped in the room from speakers connected to a hidden sound system. Off the main dining room was a tight hallway housing two bathrooms. Beyond that the hallway led to the garden patio area with a larger stage for entertainment. On Sunday evening this was the only place in downtown Fairhope, Alabama open and definitely the only place to get a drink after 9pm.

The barstools were mostly empty at the rail so she walked over, taking a seat at the corner of the bar. Ophelia looked around to see maybe a dozen customers all casually dressed, she felt out of place in her clothes, of course she did. Dressed in her navy blue suit, white dress shirt and hair in a loose bun, she screamed banker; but at 9 o'clock on Sunday night, maybe 'FBI agent' was blaring from her clothes. It was a small town, her family was well known and so most everyone knew she had returned and what she was doing for a living. The Griffin family was old Mobile, Alabama money. Her great grandfather on her father's side had two cotton plantations way back when and that money had trickled down to the present time. After her father's passing three years ago, the money was now hers. She had a trust fund with access at 21 but never needed to utilize the money. Her parents were modest for the most part, both high school teachers. They brought her up right. She was every bit a class act with manners, loyal to friends, and a hard worker. When speaking to her, her education was more noticeable than her money; which would make her parents proud.

In the most southern accent she had heard all day the bartender asked, "What can I get you, sweetheart?"

Ophelia forced a smile, "Goose and Soda with a lime, thank you."

Ophelia was thankful her southern dialect had faded tremendously from her time in DC and New York, but returning to the south she caught herself falling into the southern speak, which made her cringe when hearing her own voice. Her drink arrived and she performed her usual squeeze of lime, quick sip and long pull. Her lips burned a bit but it was a better feeling than the tightness in her chest she felt over returning to Fairhope, Alabama.

"Lord have mercy, is that Ophelia Griffin sittin' at my bar?"

Ophelia looked up from the Fox News she was reading on her phone screen to see tall, dark, handsome and grade-school super villain.

"Since when is this your bar?" Ophelia raised her eyebrow looking at Seth Corrigan.

"I bought it from my Daddy last year. I heard you were blessing Fairhope with your presence. How's the FBI?" Seth asked, dragging out the letters of her place of employment and adding a thick southern twang.

"Just fine, thank you. I thought you were teaching, not tending bar?" Ophelia was quick to respond.

She knew Seth had purchased the bar, since she spoke to his sister

Shelby several times a week, but Ophelia didn't want him to think she kept up on what was happening in his life just because his sister was her best friend.

"Professor by day, handsome bartender at night," Seth said with dancing eyebrows.

Ophelia rolled her eyes, "Some things never change." She looked back to her phone, picking up her rocks glass and touching it to her lips. He was as full of himself as always.

Seth chuckled, "Ain't that the truth, I'm surprised your eyes haven't rolled to the back of your head and stayed there."

She placed her phone on the bar and gave Seth a scowl, "You've always thought you were a comedian. Hasn't anyone told you that you're not funny?" She noticed he used 'ain't' and figured it was just to annoy her. They had an argument in grade school that southern dialect doesn't excuse proper English.

"People find me down right entertainin'. Maybe it's you?"

Seth stood in front of her with his hands in the front pockets of his jeans. The denim slouched slightly but showed his muscular thighs and when she took a sip of her drink, Ophelia noticed that he still looked good, downright gorgeous. She figured he must still be a runner like he was in high school and college.

She met his eyes, "Why are you pestering me?"

The twinkle in his eyes was charming but she didn't want to admit it, she didn't even want to like him. The only reason to talk to him was the relationship she had with his sister and parents.

"Pestering?" He gave her a half grin, "How are you adjusting from your big city life? I heard you are staying in town? Why not the bay house?" Seth asked with curiosity. Ophelia was staying in a rental and not her family home on the bay. The house had been vacant since her father's death. Sitting on the bay the view was beautiful from her back deck, like his parents' bay house just a quarter mile down the road.

"I'm adjusting. I miss DC and my friends. Living in town is easier. When did you come back for good? What happened to California?" She questioned, figuring if she was forced to have a conversation, it was going to be direct and she would put him on the spot like he was doing to her.

Shelby had given her the reader's digest version of his coming back to Fairhope but she was interested in the details.

"I moved back almost three years ago. I didn't love California."

Ophelia nodded her head, "Why didn't you love it?"

Seth ignored her question, "Don't you think you are a little overdressed for the bar?"

"I was working and stopped for a drink on my way home," Ophelia answered with little interest in continuing the conversation. She picked her phone up reading the incoming text message. The message was from her ex-boyfriend. She wasn't going to respond but hoped reading the message would give Seth the hint that she was done talking to him.

Seth watched her put her phone down, not answering whoever was on the other end, "How's the U.S. Attorney General? Glad to be back in Alabama?" Seth really didn't care but was interested in finding out if Ophelia was back for good. He also wanted to keep the conversation going.

"Alabama is the family's home, they love it here." Ophelia didn't look at Seth, instead she picked her phone up and read another text.

"But you don't?" Seth inquired with a raised eyebrow.

Ophelia sighed and looked up, "I have a love-hate relationship with Alabama these days. I'm not thrilled to be back in the south. This wasn't part of my plan." Ophelia was finished with her drink and pushed the glass forward. She put her phone in her purse readying herself to leave.

Seth was quick to make her another drink, "Stay for one more, I'm coming around to join you." He placed her drink on the napkin in front of her and a beer and napkin in front of the seat next to her.

"I work early," Ophelia informed him.

Seth ignored her and walked to the other end of the bar to exit and come around to the customer side. When he sat down next to her, she got a whiff of his cologne. Annoyed, she thought, *Dear God why does he have to smell good?* In her mind, she chanted to herself, *I do not like Seth Corrigan. I do not like Seth Corrigan.*

Seth enjoyed being close enough to study her face. Looking in her eyes was almost too much for him, he could get lost in the blue. The last time he sat this close was three years ago and her eyes were so sad he hated to think of the image. Now they had a look of annoyance, but beautiful, blue annoyance.

He smiled at her, "Still with your FBI boyfriend?" Again stretching out the letters of her place of employment when he spoke.

Ophelia was sipping her drink and almost choked.

"Yeah, I heard you had a serious thing going," Seth answered the question before she spoke. He took a drink of his beer. His sister had told him that she dumped the boyfriend but didn't share the details.

"My relationship with Nick ended a couple months ago. He wasn't exactly interested in Alabama and I wasn't exactly interested in him anymore." Ophelia gave a half smile, "I guess your sister likes to share a little too much."

Seth nodded, "You talk to my sister all the time; she can't keep a secret. Plus my mom visits your mom, so I guess you can say your name comes up."

Ophelia knew his mom visited her mom; she talked with Mrs.

Corrigan after each visit. Her mother wasn't a topic she was going to discuss tonight.

Ophelia figured she already knew the answer but asked anyway, "What about you? Still dating every girl in town?"

Seth's head shook a little and he smirked, "I date. Not every girl in town." He raised an eyebrow with a half smirk knowing that was an unkind remark and added, "I'm not serious with anyone. I'm content with teaching and my extra time is devoted to this place right now."

Ophelia's second drink only had a sip or two missing when she said, "I really need to get going." Ophelia pushed her stool back and stood.

Seth stood when she did. That was the way a man behaved in the south. He was a bit nervous but with the confidence he had in his good looks and southern charm he said, "I haven't seen you around town much. Why don't you come in on Wednesday evening? A group of friends are meeting me to listen to the band. I will re-introduce you to some school friends and maybe you can get out of this work get up?" Seth was looking at her again with a twinkle in his eye that she now decided was pure meanness.

"Let me think…" Ophelia said, and toying with him she put her finger on her chin, "NO!" She shook her head with a cocky smirk. Seth looked at her shocked so Ophelia gave him an explanation, "Moving back here has been hard enough. I don't need you making it worse by having a bunch of your friends make fun of me. Heaven knows you took great pride in that when we were young. I'm more than capable of re-introducing myself if I care to."

Seth laughed, "Really? You're still holding a grudge?"

Ophelia thought back to when she was 13 years old. On the particular morning that flashed in her mind, Ophelia stepped on the school bus to 20 children making a howling sound like a fire engine, only to have Seth Corrigan stand up and yell, 'She's on fire, put her out'. That was 16 years ago and the memory was still fresh and one of her least favorites. Seth enjoyed tormenting her, being two years older and beyond popular, most everyone followed him blindly. So if Seth made fun of her, everyone else did too. Ophelia turned a soft shade of pink from embarrassment just thinking about the incident. The teasing was in reference to her red hair. Sixteen years ago she was one of the only redheads in Fairhope, besides her Momma. She hated being different back then and it was a perfect reason for children to be mean. Once she was in High School and College, she knew having red hair was one of her better assets and felt blessed for the red locks. Her red hair got her noticed with men falling over themselves to touch it or ask her out on dates because of it.

Ophelia looked him straight in the eyes, "She's on fire, put her out?" Ophelia's face still tinted pink had an unpleasant look of disgust for him when she said with snark, "I have to hand it to you, you knew how to make 13 even more awkward. You were a horrible child; I doubt much has changed." Ophelia looked down locating her purse strap and put it over her shoulder.

Seth's voice was a little gentler, "Come on. I was 15 and of course a shit. Most boys are at that age." He couldn't help but touch her hair to tuck a few loose strands behind her ear. "You know how beautiful your hair is. You are not short on being complimented, never were. The awkward wore off by high school."

"Still I'm sure you have been scheming new ways to torture me. I'll pass," Ophelia had already moved away from his touch, stepping back from her barstool when she delivered her comment.

Seth chuckled, "I think you are a little conceited. I have quite a bit to think about besides plotting the teasing of Ophelia Griffin.

What? Are you scared a big city girl like yourself can't hang with us southern folk anymore?"

Ophelia rolled her eyes, "Please, do you think I'm 5 years old? Dangle a 'you're scared and can't handle it' comment and I'll accept? What kind of girls have you been hanging out with anyway? Obviously not the smart kind." Ophelia waited for half a second, enjoying his look of bewilderment at the NO she delivered, clearly he wasn't use to being denied anything from a girl. She smirked, "By the look on your face, you don't get turned down very often." She turned away from him. Before taking a step towards the door to leave, she looked over her shoulder, "Good night. Always a pleasure."

Seth sat back down on the barstool. He knew it was not her pleasure; at least not yet.

CHAPTER 2

Ophelia reported to work at 6am on Monday morning. U.S. Attorney General James Sipes' home was a large five bedroom sitting on about an acre of land. The Sipes family received around the clock protection. Ophelia worked mostly with Mrs. Sipes and their daughters Caroline and Clara. The girls were five and seven years old. Ophelia had a wonderful relationship with the family, having been their protection for nearly three years. Mrs. Sipes personally asked her to come with them to Fairhope. The Attorney General had ambitions of running for President in the future. To build a solid foundation for a presidential run, it was recommended that he become an elected official. His plan was to finish his term as Attorney General and run for Governor in Alabama. This would keep the family in Fairhope where Mrs. Sipes' parents lived.

"Good Morning, Agent Griffin." AG Sipes nodded with a smile holding a bottle of water, dressed in work out clothes.

"Good Morning, Sir. Looks like it will be a beautiful day. Enjoy your run." Ophelia replied with a warm smile. Walking to the small office off the entrance to the home, she checked in with the additional FBI security on staff.

"Hey Mark, any word on Christmas?" Ophelia was curious what the plans were for the holiday. They had a little more than three weeks to get travel organized.

"Yes, just heard, Vermont, skiing," Mark answered with a full on grin.

Ophelia shook her head, "That made you happy."

Mark nodded, "I love skiing."

"Let me know what you need from me. I'm going to check on the girls." Ophelia headed to the staircase. Two little girls started down the stairs ready for school. "You both look lovely today," Ophelia complimented both girls.

"Miss Ophelia, do you like my pretty dress?" Five-year-old Caroline asked.

"Of course you look like the belle of the ball," Ophelia smiled at Caroline and looked to Clara, "Very pretty hairdo, Clara."

"Thank you, Miss Ophelia."

The girls were followed down the stairs by Mrs. Sipes, "Good morning, Ophelia."

"Good Morning, Mrs. Sipes. Is there anything you need?"

"Just to get these monkeys some breakfast," Mrs. Sipes answered following the girls to the kitchen.

For the most part, Ophelia followed a specific daily routine. She accompanied Mrs. Sipes and the girls to school in the morning, spent the day protecting Mrs. Sipes if she was out of the house, and picked up the girls from school. She attended social outings and appointments with Mrs. Sipes in the evenings when needed. On occasion she was on the AG's detail depending on the family's needs. Ophelia enjoyed protecting the family and knew she would be sad for the assignment to end. When the Attorney General's term was complete the following year, his FBI protection would end. If Sipes won Governor of Alabama he would hire private protection or the State Police would be assigned to the family. If indeed he did run for the presidency, Secret Service would step in to protect him and his family during the campaign. This would be the last year with the Sipes family, which made Ophelia a little anxious about what was next. She would have choices with the FBI but wasn't sure what she wanted for her future.

By the time Wednesday rolled around, Ophelia was interested in trying out a bit of a social life. She thought about letting Seth know she was planning on stopping at the bar but decided against it. What would it matter since she was joining a group of friends? Plus she didn't want to call his sister for his phone number. Ophelia walked in Bone and Barrel wearing a form fitting, black, v-neck, knit sweater, dark blue jeans and high-heeled black ankle boots. Her red hair was long and flowing with soft spiral waves to the middle of her back, and she had long bangs that swooped to the left and tucked behind her ear if needed. Ophelia stood 5'10 with her heels and was every bit a knock out. She always wore the perfect amount of make-up, never over done. Looking around the inside seating she didn't see Seth or anyone that would be in his group of friends that looked familiar, so she proceeded to the bar to get a drink before walking to the back patio area. With her corona with lime in one hand and her Gucci clutch in the other, she walked closer to the patio so she was able to hear the band. It was 8:30pm; she figured the band had been playing for about 30 minutes. She liked the idea she was fashionably late, plus she wanted to make sure Seth wouldn't think she was eager for socializing.

"Ophelia!" A dyed blond yelled with excitement causing Ophelia to turn her head to the right.

"Michelle, how are you?" Ophelia smiled and approached a high school friend giving her a hug. Michelle was a brunette in high school but the blond hair was pretty.

"Come join us. Seth was hoping you would get off work and join us tonight," Michelle pulled up a chair next to hers while speaking.

Ophelia looked around the table saying 'Hi' to everyone. When she met Seth's eyes she said, "Hi," giving him a nice smile that he returned.

Two hours passed quickly and her mouth and ears were exhausted; the group had talked her to death. They had all shared what they had been doing and asked her a million questions about her life in New York and Washington.

"I had a great time. It was so nice to see all of you but I have to get going. I'm working early," Ophelia said with sincerity giving Michelle a hug good-bye and waving to everyone else at the table.

"Come out with us tomorrow night," Michelle called after her.

"I've got your phone number. Let me see if I can work it out; I'll call if I can," Ophelia nodded with a smile. She wasn't sure she wanted to commit to two nights in a row.

Ophelia walked through the hallway and into the main dining area where she was stopped by a 20 something year old guy who was quick to ask for her phone number and she was quick to deny. Seth was behind her and watched with amusement. He let her make it out the front door before he said her name.

"Phe," Seth called her name nickname, only a few steps behind her.

Ophelia turned, "I knew it was you, not many people call me that," she said, giving her eyebrows a bounce. She wondered what he had in store for her.

"I like to think I'm special," he winked.

"Did you follow me out here to tell me how special you are?" she said with a little flirt to her voice.

"I figured you just knew that." Seth raised an eyebrow flirting back, "I followed you out here to ask if you wanted to come out tomorrow night. I know Michelle mentioned it; it will be a great time. We are all going to Daphne for a holiday event. Why don't you join us?" Seth hoped she would go.

"I don't know. I appreciate the invitation but I think I'll take a rain check." "Why? There was no teasing and you had a good time tonight. You smiled quite often and I think you may have laughed a time or two." Seth enjoyed watching her, her smile was beautiful and the way her lips moved when she spoke turned him on.

"I enjoyed myself. Thank you for inviting me. If I can swing it tomorrow night, I'll get a hold of someone and find out where everyone is and meet up."

Seth shook his head, "No point in driving to Daphne when I'm going the same direction. I'll pick you up at 5:30pm. You are staying in the Callahan house in the Fruit and Nut district, right?" Seth was easy to talk to and well liked so his customers were never quiet about what was happening around town.

Ophelia looked at him surprised.

"I own a bar. Everyone sits at the rail and talks; it's a small town. Plus you are not too far from my place." Seth explained.

She laughed, "I thought I was the FBI agent, looks like you are doing some pretty good investigation work yourself."

"No, no," he laughed, "You coming back to town with the AG has people talking a bit. What do you say, tomorrow night? Come on, we are all friends."

"Fine. I'll see you at 5:30," Ophelia agreed.

Ophelia was completely ready to walk out the door when Seth arrived. She was nervous and didn't want to linger at the rental. Her luggage was still packed; she was living out of the suitcases due to being unsure of her next move. Ophelia knew Seth would make a comment or have an opinion about her not living at the bay house and didn't want to have that conversation. She didn't want him telling his parents she hadn't really moved in.

When she heard him knock, Ophelia opened the door with a pretty smile, "Hi."

Seth's eyes took a good look at her while he stumbled over his hello. Her hair was down with soft curls at the ends that fell on her form fitted sage green sweater. She wore sexy skinny jeans tucked in to high-heeled brown leather boots. She carried a small clutch and winter vest. Fairhope's weather in early December would be in the 50's and tonight was no exception.

"Hi. Ready to go?" Seth's smile was large.

"Sure am," Ophelia answered and walked out of the door, locking it behind her.

Seth followed her off the porch, escorting her to the car and opening the door. When he closed the passenger car door, she watched him walk around the front of the car. Seth was a man that turned a woman's head. He filled out jeans perfectly and his chest and arms begged for touching. His smoldering green eyes smiled when he spoke, and she didn't even want to start thinking about his lips and perfect teeth. Seth Corrigan had a reputation as a heartbreaker and ladies man with the looks to prove it. His short dark wavy hair literally called your fingers to dig in and enjoy. She shook her head to clear her thoughts.

"I'm starving, have you been to Dragonfly Food Bar? I want to feed you the best Ahi tacos in town," Seth smiled pulling out of her driveway.

"I haven't been there yet." Ophelia looked concerned, "I thought we were heading to Daphne to meet everyone."

"We are but we need to grab something to eat," He confirmed.

Dragonfly Food Bar was a unique tapas restaurant that served tacos and rice bowls with both a Mexican and Asian taste. The restaurant was funky with patio seating warmed by outdoor heaters that Seth and Ophelia enjoyed.

"You're right, these are the best Ahi tacos I've ever had. I love the little kick of wasabi," Ophelia complimented before eating the last of her second taco.

"I know right?" Seth looked at his watch, "Ok we have to go." He signaled for the waitress to come over and gave her his credit card.

"You shouldn't get mine," Ophelia said reaching for her purse.

"Are you forgetting where you are? In the south and with me, you don't pay," Seth said taking the final bite of his fourth taco and washing it down with a drink of his beer.

Ophelia smiled and thanked him, but wasn't comfortable with him paying. She didn't want this to resemble a date.

The drive between Fairhope and Daphne was normally 10 minutes but since they were driving during rush hour with people coming home from work, traffic would cause them at least a 30-minute drive.

"Thank you for dinner," Ophelia offered again.

"Two tacos and a corona is not exactly a dinner," Seth chuckled.

Ophelia fidgeted a bit, blurting out, "Look I want to say something just to get it out there. I appreciate you paying but I don't expect you to do that. I see the way you've been looking at me and I'm not interested in dating or getting involved. I'm here for work and need to concentrate on that." She wasn't sure that was exactly true but didn't want to be played around by ladies man Seth Corrigan, no matter how attracted she was to him.

Seth contemplated for a moment as to his reply. "Well, I wouldn't read much into the way I've been looking at you. I am a man and can appreciate a beautiful woman without wanting to get involved. And I don't want to date you or get romantically involved with you either.

I'm only offering friendship, so stop being so full of yourself." He gave her a smirk, happy with his quick comeback and to drive the point home he focused on the road, not giving her a glance.

"Good," Ophelia's voice sounded sort of miffed. She was annoyed he didn't want to date her even though she didn't want to date him.

"Fine," Seth replied aggravated that she picked up on his obvious interest. The truth was he was interested in dating her but had plans to take it slow and let them get to know each other again. He had been interested in dating Ophelia Griffin since he was 17 years old, when her daddy told him he was too old for her at that time. Once they were in college they went their separate ways and now that she was back, it was his chance.

The awkward silence was broken when Ophelia said, "What kind of holiday event are we going to in Daphne?"

Seth's smile filled his face. He was going to take great enjoyment in her reaction, "We are going to dress like Christmas Elves and go on a bike ride through downtown."

Ophelia laughed, "Hell no, I'm not. You planned for us to ride bikes and let me where these high heels? What? You saved up all the humiliation for tonight? Luring me here after I had a pleasant time last night?"

Seth laughed, "Yes, I let you wear those heels because I like them. You look sexy wearing them. What can I say, I'm a man. Plus, I figured with you being an FBI agent and all, you're resourceful and can figure it out."

"Looks like I'm plum out of an Elf costume so I'll just wait for you at the bar," Ophelia chuckled.

"Got it covered. Shelby said you were six on the bottom and eight on the top. I got your hat and ears and everything." Seth was resourceful as well.

"You knowing my size is a little too personal don't you think?" Ophelia raised an eyebrow.

Seth chuckled, "I'm not going to help you get dressed, just going to hand you the clothes." Seth gave her a quick and flirty look, "That is unless you need me to help you take something off."

"I don't think so," Ophelia rolled her eyes with a laugh.

Seth changed the subject, "What happened between you and Nick? You said it ended a few months ago, was it because you decided to come back to Fairhope?" Seth wanted the details his sister neglected to share about Ophelia's ex-boyfriend.

Ophelia shook her head, "No, we had already broken up two months before I left DC."

Seth was still driving but glanced her way for just a second and gestured with a forward motion with his hand for her to go on.

Ophelia continued with reluctance, "I'm surprised your sister didn't tell you all the details," Ophelia said, stalling and looking at him, but he just gave her the gesture to go on. She rolled her eyes, "I don't know. A lot happened between us. After my daddy's funeral and hearing about everyone getting married, I felt really alone. I ended up moving from New York to DC taking me away from my friends and to the assignment to protect the AG and his family. I met Nick at work and he was from the North, different from every boy I had ever dated. He was fun and fast and I wanted to be with someone, probably more than wanting to be with the right someone. I overlooked things that I shouldn't have. We ended up living together about a year in and that's when things started getting difficult. He was doing some extensive traveling for work and when he would come home he was suspicious of what I had been doing. He was checking my phone and reading my text messages. He had accused me of being interested in other men. I didn't give him a reason to feel insecure and the more insecure he became the less I liked him. I started wondering if the reason he was accusing me was because he was doing things he shouldn't. So we had a few horrible arguments and finally I asked him to move out."

Seth nodded with a look of concern, "How did he take it?"

Ophelia shrugged, "He was upset. Still is. He sent me a message last week that he needs to talk to me. I didn't respond. I've said all I'm going to."

"I'm sure he was upset. I can't imagine he would be happy about losing you. Was he cheating?" Seth asked.

"I don't know. I thought that a couple women we worked with were a little too friendly and familiar for co-workers. Honestly, it was over and it didn't matter so I didn't ask," Ophelia said with a sad smile.

"That sucks. I'm really sorry. Are you ok with how things turned out?" Seth glanced her way.

"Yes, I'm good," Ophelia nodded. "What I realized was that I never missed him when he traveled for work. I didn't love Nick, at least not the way my parents loved each other. We weren't right."

Ophelia started paying attention to the road where they were turning in to park. The streets were decorated with Christmas lights and the parking lot had tons of people dressed like elves standing next to bicycles.

Seth smiled, "Let's go spread some Christmas cheer."

Ophelia could help the smile that reached all the way to her eyes.

Ophelia used the ladies room in Manci's Antique Club to change her clothes and after she walked towards Seth, who was waiting at the tandem bike they would be riding together.

"Wow. This bike makes a statement," Ophelia put her hand over her mouth hiding her laugh, "and so do you," Ophelia giggled.

The tandem bike was flashing with red and green lights. Seth was dressed like an elf, ears, and bells on his turned up shoes. Seth turned in a circle showing off his outfit.

Seth twirled his hand around motioning for her to twirl around, "Show off your elf style."

Ophelia turned in her green dress with the red and green striped stockings. Her elf hat was trimmed with a white fluffy rim that hung above her eyebrows. She curtsied at the end of her twirl. Seth's heart raced. Ophelia was very cute in the costume and he laughed to himself that he could be turned on looking at her dressed like an elf.

The bikes took off riding the downtown streets of Daphne. Ophelia was behind Seth on the tandem bike managing to toss candy to the spectators lining both sides of the street.

"How's it going back there?" Seth turned his head to see Ophelia smiling.

"You're doing most of the work. I'm having so much fun," she said with excitement.

At the end of the ride the participants gathered near the 15 foot Christmas tree for prizes to be handed out for best male elf, female elf and decorated bicycle.

The group of friends pulled together two tables at Manci's Antique Club. The bar had amazing po'boys and the loaded fries would bring you to your knees. They ordered drinks and toasted to The Elf Ride and friendship. Ophelia completely enjoyed herself. She was comfortable around Seth, more so than she thought she would or should be. It was easy to be with him. They found themselves laughing and enjoying each other's company, not needing to rely on the rest of the group. She noticed that he touched her often, sometimes on her lower back when they walked into the bar and sometimes he tucked her hair behind her ear. Many times when he spoke he would touch her arm. It seemed natural for him to do those things, almost like he wasn't thinking about it. She tried not to question the touching because they both said they were not interested in each other. Maybe he just felt comfortable and since they knew each other since childhood, he had touched her a million times. The problem was that now that they were adults, his touch put her body on high alert. Ophelia had always been attracted to Seth; she didn't want to be but there was no denying it. Her body wouldn't let her.

"I had the best time. Thank you. If you wouldn't have pushed me to come with you, I would have missed out." Ophelia had a large smile on her face as they walked back to the car. "Thank you for the elf costume." She was carrying it in her arms after changing back into her jeans and sweater.

"I'm glad you had fun. I did too." Seth opened her car door, letting her get in and closed it.

When he started the car, Ophelia giggled, "Seriously that was the best time. I didn't think I was going to have that much fun."

He smiled wide, happy that she had enjoyed herself. "I think you make a great partner in crime. We were definitely the best on the tandem bikes."

Ophelia laughed, "Don't tell the FBI I'm a great partner in crime."

"Your secrets safe."

They were quiet for a few moments and Ophelia asked, "So what happened in California? I know you were offered a job with the NSA and you had a girlfriend but then you moved back."

Seth raised his eyebrows, "That's a story that deserves a beer." The truth was he didn't want to talk about it.

"Ok. Let's have a beer." Ophelia gave him a gentle smile.

"Don't you need to get to bed? You work early." Seth was hoping to put that story off forever if possible.

"I don't think a beer will hurt. Besides I shared, it's your turn. I'll even buy the beer." Ophelia smiled.

"You don't buy my beer. We already went over that tonight. I need to stop and check on the bar. Are you ok with getting a beer there?" Seth asked.

"Sure." Ophelia agreed.

Ophelia took a seat at a table away from the ears of the bartender. She watched Seth talk to some of the staff while he retrieved two beers out of the cooler. He walked over and sat across from her, handing her a beer.

"Thank you. Cheers," Ophelia said, clinking the neck of her beer with his and taking a drink. "Did they have a good night?"

"Yes, we had a good dinner crowd." Seth smiled, "This place has been doing really well."

"That's good to hear. Does your dad like being retired?" Ophelia asked.

"I don't know if you can call him retired. He's pretty busy." Seth smiled, "But he likes that his time is his own."

Ophelia smiled but felt sad. She missed her father.

Seth noticed the look on Ophelia's face and changed the subject to one that would bring the sad face to him instead of her, "So I guess you want to hear about my California life?" Seth raised an eyebrow.

Ophelia smiled giving him the same 'go on' gesture he had given her earlier.

"Berkley was great for my Master's Degree. They have the best Data Science program in the country and that was what I thought I wanted. What I came to understand was what you are good at and what you have a passion for are two different things sometimes. The job offer with the NSA was flattering but what I really wanted was to be a teacher. I have always wanted to be a teacher. That is what inspires me; what I'm passionate about. So instead of taking the NSA job I started applying for teaching jobs. Carolyn, my girlfriend while I was at Berkley and beyond, was not thrilled that I didn't take the NSA job and when I say not thrilled I mean she was unhappy with me. She wanted to have a specific kind of life and I wasn't meeting those expectations. I was unhappy in California and since she wasn't happy with me anyway, I told her I wanted to come back to Alabama and teach. I asked her to come with me; she didn't want to leave California. We tried the long distance thing but it ended when I caught her sleeping with one of my friends on a surprise visit." Seth took a big drink of his beer.

"Ouch. I'm sorry." Ophelia said feeling hurt for him.

"The thing was, I knew we weren't going to make it before I came back. Carolyn worked from home for an IT company; she could work from anywhere. Coming with me for just a semester to see if she liked Fairhope was doable, she just didn't want to," Seth shrugged.

"Do you think you were testing her?" Ophelia asked.

Seth raised an eyebrow, "Maybe. I didn't think it was the forever kind of love and I ended up being right."

Ophelia gave a half smile, "Are you ok with it?"

Seth nodded, "Yes. It's been three years. I love teaching. I feel fulfilled; I'm where I'm supposed to be. Fairhope has always been home to me."

Ophelia smiled, "It must be nice to have your career figured out. I don't yet."

"I thought you enjoyed toting a gun and flashing your badge?" Seth smirked.

"Very funny. I enjoy protecting the AG's family and I liked the investigation work when I was in the New York field office but this assignment will end and I'm not sure what's next," Ophelia explained, taking a drink of her beer.

"So the rumors in the political arena are true? Sipes is going to run for Governor?"

"They aren't rumors anymore. He announced," Ophelia confirmed. "Once his term as A.G. is over, he will hire private security and I'll be reassigned."

"Are you going to stay here?" Seth asked.

Ophelia shrugged, "I don't know. I have that love hate thing with Alabama."

Seth smiled and shook his head, "You haven't spent any time doing the things you loved here. You loved Fairhope. I remember you saying you were going to open a law office somewhere on the street."

Ophelia smiled, "A lot has changed. That seems like a very long time ago."

"You're still a lawyer. That hasn't changed. It wasn't so long ago." Seth added.

"I'm still a lawyer. I'm not the same girl," Ophelia said taking the last drink of her beer.

"I think you are," Seth's eyes searched hers, finding the fire in them that had always been there. *She was the same girl, maybe she didn't want to be but...* he let the thought trail off, "I should get you home." Seth took the final drink of his beer. He collected the bottles from the table and said good night to his staff.

They pulled up in the driveway at the rental house Ophelia was staying in. She looked at him, "Thank you again."

"I'll walk you to the door." Seth got out of the car and walked around to her side, opening the car door.

When they reached the porch, Ophelia had her keys in her hand. She was nervous that he walked her to the door.

She turned to him, "I had a great time; I'll see you soon."

Seth watched her lips move as she spoke and had the urge to brush his lips to hers but he didn't. Instead he said, "I did too. Thanks for going tonight." He wrapped his arms around her and hugged her close.

Ophelia hugged him back, loving how she fit. When she walked in the house and shut the door behind her she decided that she needed to stay away from Seth. She enjoyed being with him too much and no matter what they said, the chemistry and the looks that they were sharing were nothing but trouble in the making.

CHAPTER 3

Ophelia was sad and uncomfortable sitting on the porch with her mother.

"It's been a beautiful day, hasn't it Ma'am?" Ophelia asked with a smile.

She loved to hear her mother's voice, something that hadn't changed. She knew calling her "Momma", which was what she wanted and needed to do, would send her mother into a panicked confusion that would end in hysteria and medication pushed by syringe into her mother to calm her.

"It is sugar. Which patient are you visiting today? Are you sure they don't mind me taking up your time?"

"No Ma'am, there is plenty of my time to share." Ophelia smiled.

The conversation went on for about an hour about flowers, the weather, and anything that was easy and didn't require Ellie to know who Ophelia was.

"Darlin', I have taken up enough of your time. You should go enjoy your family," Ellie smiled looking at Ophelia affectionately.

"Yes Ma'am. Why don't I walk in with you?"

Ophelia and her mother were buzzed in the door. Ellie followed Ophelia down the hall to the community room. Ophelia turned to see Ellie smiling and ready to join the other patients.

"It was nice visiting with you. May I hug you good bye?" Ophelia knew to ask so that Ellie would stay relaxed.

"I would like that." Ellie wrapped her arms around Ophelia.

The hug was for Ophelia so she could smell her mother's hair. Her mother didn't need the embrace and probably would have preferred not to be touched which was the opposite of how she was before the disease took over.

Ophelia mouthed without sound, 'I love you Momma'.

Ellie broke the embrace walking in the community room not looking back. Ophelia stood watching her mother and wiped the tears from the corners of her eyes. Every visit was difficult. Her mother never knew who she was but sometimes like today she would let Ophelia close to her as a stranger.

"Good visit today?" One of the nurses smiled approaching Ophelia.

Ophelia smiled slightly with a nod, "Yes, she's doing well today."

"And you? How are you?"

Ophelia shrugged, "Best I can. Thank you for asking."

Ophelia left Homestead Village of Fairhope heading to the parking lot when she saw Mom Corrigan, Seth and Shelby's Mother, walking towards her. She was greeted with a big hug.

"Mom Corrigan, it's so good to see you. I'm sorry I haven't been by to visit you and Dad Corrigan yet."

"That's ok. We know you've been getting settled. I insist you come to dinner Sunday. I've missed this beautiful face." Mom Corrigan smiled touching Ophelia's cheek. She could tell Ophelia's eyes were glassy from the visit with her mother, "How was she today?"

"Ok. She let me talk to her." Ophelia offered a small smile.

Mom Corrigan kissed Ophelia's cheek, "You are a wonderful

daughter."

Ophelia hugged Mom Corrigan again so she could hide the anguish on her face.

A bottle of wine and a large bouquet of flowers were in Ophelia's arms when she knocked on the door of the Corrigan's bay house. The house was high on stilts with about 25 stairs to climb to the door. It sat on Mobile Bay over looking the water. She had been to the house a million times as a young girl. She and Shelby were inseparable all through their childhood. The ocean was a big part of their lives so this bay house and her parents bay house were the places to be all summer. The docks housed jet skis and boats. They fished and set crab traps. Living by the ocean was an amazing life. Ophelia's best childhood memories were shared with the Corrigan family. The door opened with Seth standing on the other side.

He grinned, "You shouldn't have."

Ophelia's smile faded, "I didn't. I thought you worked on Sundays?"

"I heard you were coming to dinner so, here I am."

Ophelia rolled her eyes, "Three times in one week. I think I might be on Seth overload."

Mom Corrigan pushed Seth out of the way; "Go help your father with the grill." Mom Corrigan smiled at Ophelia, "Come in sweetheart. I did teach him manners, he just chooses not to use them."

Seth chuckled, "I was inviting her in, you didn't give me a chance. Why doesn't Ophelia have to help with the grill?"

Mom Corrigan hugged Ophelia, "Because she was invited and you intruded."

Ophelia laughed.

"Come on let's have a glass of wine and sit on the back porch while the men finish grilling." Mom Corrigan led the way to the kitchen where she poured two glasses of wine.

Ophelia followed her to the back porch. It was screened in, overlooking the ocean. The view was breathtaking just like it was at her parent's house.

"I love it here. Shelby and I would camp out on this back porch when we were little. Some of my favorite memories." Ophelia stood, walking to the screened window looking out over the water.

Mom Corrigan smiled, "I always think that salt air and the sound of the ocean can fix most things."

Ophelia didn't look back just said, "Most things."

Seth was standing watching her look out and interrupted, "Dinner is ready."

Dinner was delicious with everyone enjoying fresh fish, red potatoes and grilled vegetables. The conversation was enjoyable with the Corrigan parents asking questions about Ophelia's work and the Sipes daughters.

"I'm probably a little too attached. It's hard not to be. They are the sweetest little girls." Ophelia's face lit up when she talked about them.

"Would you consider staying on as private security when he makes a run for Governor?" Dad Corrigan asked.

Ophelia shook her head, "No, I'm not going to go private security. I'll see what the next assignment is and make decisions based on that."

Dad Corrigan followed up, "There's always the Mobile or Pensacola field offices," he suggested, wanting Ophelia to stay close.

Ophelia nodded, taking a sip of her wine. She didn't know that she would be interested and it was far enough off that a serious conversation wasn't warranted yet.

"What's retirement like?" Ophelia smiled, looking at Dad Corrigan.

Dad Corrigan shrugged, "I need projects to keep me busy. I'm not much for the relaxin'."

Seth laughed, "I don't think what you have going on is relaxin'. You have something planned almost every day."

"What can I say? I like a full social calendar." Dad Corrigan laughed.

Mom Corrigan smiled, "Thank God he does. He would make me crazy under my feet all day. I love him but I like him out of the house a little every day."

Everyone laughed.

"Sweetheart, why aren't you living in the bay house?" Mom Corrigan asked. "I know you love the water and you love the boat. Seth could help you with the boat. We could all help with the house. Shelby will be here on the 19th; we could all come over and get you situated. We could have you moved in before Christmas."

Ophelia quickly said, "The house and boat have been looked after. I hired a company to check on things and keep up with the boat maintenance. It's just easier to stay in town right now." She shot Seth a look.

"You know I can help you go through things, make it your own." Mom Corrigan said gently. "I just want to help in any way I can."

Ophelia gave her a warm smile, "You do help me. Visiting my Momma has been a tremendous help. I don't know that I'm ready to make the house mine yet." Ophelia changed the subject, "The fish was amazing. Did you catch them today?" She looked at Dad Corrigan.

"Yes I did. Easy go of it, pretty much jumping on the dock." He chuckled.

Ophelia smiled, "Well dinner was delicious. I'm doing the dishes." She stood and started gathering plates.

"Don't be silly. I'll get them later," Mom Corrigan stated.

"You don't be silly. It will take me just a few minutes. No arguing. Plus I'm planning on having a piece of the pecan pie so I need to earn my keep," Ophelia smiled, heading towards the kitchen with a stack of dishes.

"I'll dry," Seth offered.

He walked in the kitchen after her. Ophelia started washing and rinsing the dishes putting them on the drain board. She didn't so much as look at Seth.

"Did I do something?" Seth asked.

"You're Momma would not have asked me about the bay house if you didn't say something to her," Ophelia hissed upset.

"Phe, you shouldn't be living in a rental. My Momma's right, you love the ocean. You should be in your own home."

"Don't tell me what I should be doing. You do not know me anymore. Stop calling me Phe." She was angry but kept her voice low so Seth's parents couldn't hear their conversation.

"I do know you. You haven't changed all that much, just a bigger pain in the ass. I will call you Phe because I've been calling you that since you were 10 years old. What is the problem? You come back here and talk about how you hate Alabama. I know you love it here, you have always loved living on the water."

Ophelia didn't speak to him she could feel herself getting upset. She continued to wash the dishes until she pulled the drain, letting the water out. Once the water went down she turned on the faucet, spraying the sink out. Seth watched and waited for her to say something but she didn't.

He turned her to face him trapping her between the counter and his body, "Talk to me. What is the problem with living at the bay house?"

She shook her head looking at him like he was an idiot, "I wouldn't expect you to understand how hard this is for me, to be in Fairhope. Every emotion, all my feelings about my family are raw and I..." She paused for a moment, "My mother doesn't know me. My father is gone. That house, everything about that house is a reminder of what I've lost. I would give anything, anything for one more conversation with my Momma." Tears started to fall down her cheeks. "I have to pretend to be a stranger just to have a conversation about magnolias or the weather when I visit her. If I even make an attempt to remind her of who I am she gets so confused she..." Ophelia couldn't continue to talk, giving herself a moment. She tried to stop the crying that was taking over. "I am alone. I miss my Daddy. I still need my parents and they are gone." She paused and looked at him angrily with tears flowing down her cheeks, "You couldn't just leave it alone. I told you it was easier for me to be in town, why couldn't you just leave it be?" Ophelia was almost hysterical. She pushed passed Seth, wiping her tears. "Tell your parents thank you for dinner." She collected her purse and left.

Ophelia lay on the couch with a cool washcloth over her eyes. She had a good long cry and her face was paying for it. Her skin was fair and when she cried a noticeable pink tint appeared all around her eyes. She was doing everything she could not to think about her life while she lay there. She felt as if she was spinning out of control. There was a knock on the door. Ophelia knew it would be Seth and ignored it. When he started ringing the doorbell over and over she walked over and opened the door.

"What do you want?" She said with hostility, hating that she had a complete meltdown in front of him.

"I'm an ass and I'm so sorry." He opened the screen door that separated them and pulled her to him hugging her. "I know it's hard for you and I thought being in your house would be better. You were always so happy there. I overstepped and I apologize. I was trying to help. I didn't mean to upset you or make things worse." Seth stroked her hair and he could feel her relax against him with her face embedded in his chest. "What can I do? I want to make things better for you."

Ophelia shook her head slightly as it was pressed against him, "There's nothing you can do."

"Let me come in. I want to sit with you and talk for a few minutes."

Seth moved them into the house. He sat with her on the couch continuing to hold on to her. Ophelia's cheek was pressed against his chest and he brushed her hair out of her face.

Holding her tight he said, "I miss your Momma and Daddy too. They are the reason I wanted to be a teacher. This whole town misses them." He could feel Ophelia begin to cry and held her feeling the soft movement of her body against his. "They were two of the most special people. A good mix of tough and loving. I was scared of your Mom." He laughed a little and felt her smile slightly; his fingers had been caressing her cheek. "You didn't turn your homework in late to Mrs. Griffin." He laughed a little again. "Did you know that I asked your Daddy if I could ask you to my senior prom?" Seth didn't wait for her to reply, "He told me no, that I was not to ask you. You were too young and he was not going to allow you to go anywhere with a senior boy. I wanted desperately to date you back then but your dad wasn't having any of it." He held her for a good amount of time before he said, "They both loved you so much. You were their joy, they were so proud of you. I know they would hate that you are miserable. Your parents would want you to find peace. That house has every good memory, you have to find a way to make it about the good." He felt her body quake again from crying. "It's going to be hard, but you are tough just like them." He felt her fingers crinkle his shirt holding to him. "You can do it. You're not alone. You will never be alone." Seth stroked her hair and kissed the top of her head saying, "Everything is going to be ok."

Seth didn't remember the last time he had seen Ophelia cry or be vulnerable. He remembered that he had been concerned with how strong she was at her father's funeral three years ago. She had been a rock, consoling people when really she should have been the one needing the comfort. Looking back he realized she had the weight of the world on her shoulders. Her mother in the memory care facility because of the Alzheimer's taking her mind and laying her father to rest must have been overwhelming and scary.

Nothing was said for a long time. Ophelia had stopped crying and wiped her tears. She slowly pulled away from Seth, stood and walked to the kitchen. He got up and walked behind her. She offered him a bottle of water from the refrigerator and he took it. Ophelia took a drink of the cold water and placed her bottle on the counter.

She looked at Seth, "Thank you for coming over and saying what you did, holding me," her cheeks were tinted pink. "I miss them. When my Mom was diagnosed, my Daddy handled everything. He made sure she had everything she needed. When she couldn't live in the house anymore, he visited her every day, he took care of her to the point he didn't take care of himself. When he finally called me that he wasn't feeling well, the cancer had spread everywhere. I didn't have time to even process that he had cancer and then he was gone. Three months, and he was gone. I was so mad at both of them; my Mom for causing my Dad to neglect himself, and him for ignoring all the warning signs. Being back here is bitter sweet because I love my memories and yet they hurt."

Seth nodded and placed his water bottle on the counter. He reached for her again, this time taking the side of her face tilting it so she looked at him.

"You are doing the best you can. You don't always have to be so strong, lean on the people that care about you. I know you'll find your way. I'm here for you. My whole family is here for you. Let us help you make some more good memories." He brushed his lips against hers then kissed her cheek. Seth hugged her again, holding her for a good amount of time before he spoke, "If you need anything, call me."

Seth knew it was time for him to go, any longer and he would want to stay with her and he feared where that would lead. Ophelia nodded and broke the embrace. She was ready for him to leave because any longer and she would want him to stay.

CHAPTER 4

Mid week Seth watched Ophelia walk the Attorney General's wife and daughters in and out of shops on Fairhope Avenue. He and his dad were outside on the balcony of the bar replacing the rope lighting.

"Ophelia looks very professional and a little intimidating dressed like that walking with the FBI stride," Dad Corrigan chuckled, "It's hard for me not to picture her and Shelby as little girls afraid to jump off the dock."

"They haven't been little girls in a very long time. And you're right, Ophelia carrying a gun and being responsible for protecting that family is a little intimidating," Seth agreed.

"I bet she could put you on your ass in a fight," Dad Corrigan laughed.

"Really? I don't think so. I've got her on height and weight," Seth laughed.

"Still, I'm going to ask her if she would. You've been a little too cocky lately," Dad Corrigan raised his eyebrow.

Seth stopped wrapping the lights, "What is that supposed to mean?"

"You watch yourself with that girl. I'm not sure what you think you're doing but don't mess her around."

"I'm not messing with her. We are friends."

Dad Corrigan stopped helping to look at Seth, "Now you and I both know that is not your plan. You've had that girl in your sights since forever. If you're not serious, leave her be."

"I don't think Ophelia needs you to warn me; she's completely capable of handing me my ass if need be," Seth smirked.

"I know that. But I don't want any hurt feelings for her or for you. Makes family life difficult."

"I hear you. But I am not messing her around," Seth said convincingly.

"She's not one of the girls that comes in this bar thinking you hung the moon. She's not going to put up with much."

"Dad, we are just friends."

"Really? That's how you feel? Because you haven't been able to stop watching her since we walked out here. These lights could have been done 20 minutes ago."

Seth didn't answer he just finished with the zip ties to hold the lights in place and stated, "Finished."

Seth walked in Bone and Barrel at 10:30pm on Friday night. He stopped and talked to a few customers on his way behind the bar. He spotted Ophelia at a table with two women and a man he didn't recognize, assuming they were work friends. He couldn't help but take a good look at her. Ophelia wore a black sweater that fell off her left shoulder. All he could think of was what her shoulder would taste like on his lips, which annoyed him. Being friends with her would be easy if she didn't look like she did or talk to him in that sexy voice, or if her body wasn't the way it was. When she smiled and he looked in her eyes he was gone. What had he done to himself? 'Friends?' who was he kidding; he didn't want to be her friend. Seth needed to distract himself so he got busy behind the bar making drinks and talking to customers.

"Hey, can you take a break and have a beer?" Ophelia approached the bar looking at him with a smile, "I want to introduce you to my friends."

"Sure. Give me a couple minutes to catch the bartender up. What are y'all drinkin'?"

"Just beer. We're good, just come over."

Seth finished with the drink tickets that were backed up and took shots over to Ophelia and her friends. Ophelia introduced Seth while he placed the drinks in front of everyone, giving the tray to their waitress. He shook everyone's hand saying he was pleased to meet each of them.

"This is our holiday shot, let me know what you think," Seth said raising his glass so everyone would follow. They drank the shot which was light, fun and green."

Ophelia's friend Addison asked, "What's it called?"

"The Grinch."

Addison laughed, "Good name."

Tim was next to comment, "If I order another round are they going to sneak up on us?"

Seth smiled, "Are any of you working in the morning?"

The consensus was "No," so Seth signaled for another round. "Then it doesn't matter," he smiled.

Tim nodded, "I like the way you think."

Two shots and another round of beers in, everyone was feeling loose with their tongues.

Marren, the other work friend, piped up, "So Seth, Ophelia tells us you tormented her as a child. I'd like to hear your side of things." Marren pursed her lips. Ophelia had told her all the stories and she couldn't wait to hear his thoughts behind what he did.

Seth raised an eyebrow, "She did huh?" He looked at Ophelia, delighted that he was a topic of her conversation but not thrilled it was because he teased her. "This ones pretty dramatic. It was your every day childhood teasing," Seth said with a smartass grin referencing Ophelia's inevitable exaggeration of historical events.

The entire group laughed, but it was Addison who said, "I don't think getting a woody wood pecker doll and putting it in her high school locker was normal teasing."

Everyone chuckled.

Tim included, "Or the fire engine sounds on the school bus."

Ophelia laughed, "Don't forget 'Red, Red, pee the bed.' And I'll have you know I've never peed the bed."

Seth turned a mild shade of pink, "Ok, ok, I was horrible. Clever, but horrible."

Addison laughed, "I'll give you clever with a very good imagination. I'm surprised Ophelia still speaks to you."

Seth smiled looking at her, "I am lucky she gives me the time of day."

The conversation was fun for the next hour, ending with Tim excusing himself and Marren asking that he drop her off at home. Seth sat with Ophelia and Addison for another few minutes and excused himself to check on his staff. He sent the two women another Grinch shot and a round of beers in his absence.

Addison smiled shaking her head.

"What?" Ophelia looked at her.

"Seth is some kind of yummy. That man is gorgeous and boy does he have it bad for you." Addison raised her eyebrows up and down.

"Seth and I are just friends." Ophelia objected. But if she was being honest with herself she thought and fantasized about the brush of his lips on hers from his visit the previous Sunday when she was upset. She chalked it up to him comforting her but the tingle she felt spread all over her body.

"Do you pay attention to the way he looks at you? That is not a friend. He looks at you like he could eat you up," Addison laughed, taking a drink of her beer.

"I thought so too and said something about him eyeing me. He said I shouldn't read anything into the way he looks at me, he can appreciate an attractive woman without wanting to get involved," Ophelia raised an eyebrow with a smirk on her face.

Addison laughed out loud, "Did he believe the words he was speaking?" Addison shook her head, "Men can be so stupid." Addison raised her beer.

Ophelia clinked the neck of her beer to Addison's and said, "No truer words have ever been spoken."

She giggled, but she thought that there was some truth to Seth's proclamation. They were friends, always had been and his family was what she had left in the world.

Ophelia sat back, "I'm going to have to call for a ride if we keep this up."

Addison nodded in agreement, "I say we close the place down, might as well. You are looking very sexy in your swoopy off the shoulder sweater. If it's not Seth, look at all these southern talking men in here. You could have your pick."

Ophelia busted out laughing, "You have a thing for the accent?"

"Hell yes I do. I want to take one of these boys home and let him talk to me all night." Addison laughed.

"No more shots." Ophelia chuckled.

Ophelia looked up at the man approaching the table and her smile and laughter ended immediately.

Nick Stanford, ex-boyfriend, approached the table. "Hello, Ophelia." Nick looked at Addison and nodded, "Addison." He knew Addison from D.C.

Addison looked at him, "Nick." She didn't offer a smile.

"What are you doing here?" Ophelia asked.

"I need to talk to you and since you won't return my calls or text messages, I'm here for the weekend." Nick sat down in the empty chair between the two women who were sitting across from one another.

"Me not answering your calls or messages meant that I don't want to talk to you," Ophelia said before taking a drink of her beer.

"You need to hear what I have to say. Isn't that the southern way, manners and all?" Nick looked at her sarcastically.

"Please, you don't care about manners," Ophelia shot back.

Seth noticed the tall, muscular man join Ophelia and Addison so he made his way over to the service station in earshot of Ophelia's table. He wanted to hear what was being said in case he needed to step in. He could see the change in Ophelia's body language and the look on her face was not pleasant.

"What are you doing in this town? You are wasting your time down here. This is not going to advance your career. You should be in D.C. with me." Nick spoke to her like he was scolding a child.

Ophelia could feel her blood start to boil but managed to stay calm, "You don't care about my career. I chose this. It had nothing to do with you. I want to be here with the AG and his family. I care about those people. What is wrong with it being about something more than advancement? Don't answer that because I don't care what you think. You can get your ass on a plane back to D.C. where you belong."

"Look, I didn't come down here to criticize your decision." Nick spoke gentler, "I love you. I miss you. I know if you come home we can work this out."

"You don't know the first thing about love. I was something you thought you possessed. That was never love. Go home, Nick. I am home," Ophelia looked away taking another drink of her beer.

"That's not true. I will travel less; we can work things out. I am in love with you," Nick said with a hint of annoyance that she was arguing with him.

Ophelia looked into his eyes her mouth formed a soft smile, "If you loved me, why were you fucking our co-workers?"

Nick looked shocked. Addison looked shocked. Seth, over hearing Ophelia's question looked over to see Nick's face and what his reaction would be.

Nick took a moment, "Addison, can you give us a minute?"

Ophelia cut in, "No, she doesn't need to give you a minute." She looked at Addison, "No need to get up this won't take but a second." Ophelia looked back at Nick, "Did you think I didn't know?" She waited for Nick to respond and when he didn't she said, "I can tell when a woman is more familiar than she should be with a co-worker. You slept around and had the audacity to accuse me of doing the same when you traveled? You checked my phone and emails like I was doing something wrong and all the while you were screwing women we worked with."

"Ophelia, it was not like that." Nick looked like the rug had been pulled out from under him.

"What was it like then? You tripped and your Johnson just happened to fall into her?" Ophelia smirked. "Don't embarrass yourself. Now you get up and never bother me again."

Nick looked at her, "Let me explain."

Ophelia cut him off, "If one more word comes out of your mouth, I will knock you on your ass in front of this entire bar."

Nick gave a smug look and stood, "Really?"

Ophelia stood up, "You want to try me?"

Nick looked at her for a long moment, pushed the chair away and walked out of the bar. Ophelia sat back down, pissed off. She took a drink of her beer.

Addison looked at her, "You should have taken out your gun and shot him."

Ophelia smiled and shook her head, "He wasn't worth the bullet. I need another drink."

"We need another drink and shot, I will get them," Addison stood up but Seth gestured that he had them coming.

Addison sat back down, "Want to talk about it?"

"I wasn't 100% that he was sleeping around, until the look on his face just now confirmed it. What a bastard." Ophelia gave her head a small shake.

"You didn't confront the woman at the office?" Addison asked.

"What would be the point? I wasn't in love with Nick. It was over long before he moved out. But really cheat? Break up, move out, whatever, but don't lie and cheat. I wish I would have decked him," Ophelia smiled at the server that brought another round.

"I would have loved to see him get knocked on his ass." Addison smiled.

Seth approached, "Everything ok?" He smiled.

Ophelia looked at him, "Of course. It's fine." She smiled back taking a drink of her new beer.

"So anything to worry about with him showing up at your place? How angry does he get? Is he a hitter?" He looked at Ophelia, "We now know you could be," Seth said with a smirk.

"He's more of a crier and manipulator, not a hitter. I only threatened. I didn't do it. I've never hit anyone that didn't deserve it," Ophelia joked.

Addison laughed, "He deserved it and you still showed restraint." She lifted her beer and clinked the neck of Ophelia's beer.

Seth looked at the two of them, "Neither of you are driving home. Let me know when ya'll are ready to go and I'll take you."

Addison smiled, "Thank you Seth, that is very sweet. We are planning to get completely hammered."

Seth smiled, "I think you both are well on your way."

The women sat talking and laughing for the next hour. They were approached by several men chatting them up, which made Addison very happy. Seth watched not thrilled with the attention Ophelia was getting, even though she acted very indifferent to the attention. The men struck out one after the other. What concerned Seth was that at some point a man would come along that she was interested in and how would that make him feel? After all if he was her friend, he should be happy for her. He did not want to be just her friend and he would not be happy seeing her with anyone. Seth walked over to the table looking at two women that needed sleep.

Addison looked at him, "We are definitely ready to go."

Seth walked behind them, impressed that they were standing and walking on their own with little swaying. He opened the front and back passenger doors.

"You can sit up front since your house is closer," Ophelia said getting in the back seat and laying down.

Addison laughed, "You just want to get a head start on sleeping."

"What's the harm in that? If I'm sleeping before he drops you off,

I had a fun time," Ophelia giggled sounding very southern.

Seth smiled, enjoying that her accent was back like when she lived in Fairhope full-time.

Addison giggled, "I did too."

After dropping Addison off, Seth drove to Ophelia's rental, walked around to the rear passenger door and opened it up. Ophelia was asleep. He reached in to collect her, picking her up in a cradle hold. He pushed the car door shut with his hip.

"You don't have to carry me. I can walk," Ophelia said softly as she held around his neck.

"That's ok, you don't weigh a thing." Seth smiled. He knew she was capable of walking to her door but enjoyed that she was in his arms, "Get your keys out."

When Seth stood Ophelia at the front door he could see her sway a little.

She laughed, "Whoa, I guess those Grinch drinks finally kicked in."

"I think they kicked in a while back." He smiled helping her in the door.

"Ok, I can handle it from here," Ophelia said walking towards the kitchen.

"I think I'll give you a hand. I will get you some water and where is your Advil?"

"In my suitcase. Yes, I'm living out of my suitcases," Ophelia confessed changing course walking into the bedroom of the rental. She sat on end of the bed and fell back fully dressed with her feet on the floor, "I'm exhausted. I got up at 5am and went for a run this morning."

Seth walked in the bedroom with a smile, "Ok, little girl let's get you fixed up." He took her boots off, "I like your pink socks."

"Pink is my favorite color. Nobody knows that but your sister. It's really girly and I like to be girly under my work suit so I wear pink. You probably didn't need to know all that," Ophelia said with a girly giggle.

"Come on, sit up," Seth smiled helping her sit up so he could hand her the bottle of water and two Advil.

Ophelia took the Advil and a big drink of the water and asked, "Did you like my work friends?"

Seth nodded, "Yes, they're nice. Did you work with them in D.C.?"

"Addison and Tim, yes. Marren, she is from the Mobile office." Ophelia started paying attention to what Seth was doing, "I can do that," Ophelia handed him the bottle of water and reached up, taking out her earrings that Seth was trying to remove.

"Do you have pajamas or something you want to put on?" Seth asked.

Ophelia chuckled, "You are not putting my pajamas on me." Ophelia stood up with Seth standing in front of her. He put his hands on her hips steadying her, "I was offering to get the pajamas and help you to the bathroom so you can change."

Ophelia's hands held his upper arms, she looked up at him, "I have a t-shirt in the suitcase behind you."

Seth looked at her lips and without thinking his mouth was on hers. His kiss was hungry with his lips moving over her lips, exploring every inch. He took his time in the kiss, slow and conveying how much he wanted her. One hand left her waist to hold the side of her face and neck with the tips of his fingers threading in her hair. Seth parted her lips, seeking her tongue to tangle with his and felt her touch tighten on his arms. Her hands slid up his shoulders with one moving to the back of his neck, her fingers running through his hair.

When Ophelia stepped closer, pressing her body to his, Seth's hand slid down her lower back until he had cupped the cheek of her bottom, pulling her against him. She made a soft sound in their kiss when his fingers traced down her neck to her bare shoulder. He broke the kiss to run his lips down her neck, ending with his open mouth on her shoulder, tasting her. It was just seconds and his mouth found hers again. This time Ophelia took charge of the kiss with her teeth scraping against his lower lip and her tongue finding his. Her hands ran over his chest, landing on his abdomen and feeling the muscles under his shirt. He pulled her against him again, holding her tight with one hand on her lower back and the other hand tangled in her hair with his fingers grasping the strands of red. Their bodies pressed against each other and she could feel him hard, pushing against the front of his jeans; he was hard for her and she loved it. Ophelia's hands lingered on his sides when she broke their kiss, running her open mouth with a teasing of her tongue against his neck, tasting a hint of salt.

Seth sighed and grasped her hair a little tighter with his other hand running up her hip and over the front of her sweater. His hand softly cupped her breast with his thumb running over the pucker in the fabric where her nipple was hard under his touch. Ophelia found his lips again. This time it was both of them kissing each other with aggressive, wanting lips, their tongues diving deep and taking each other's breath with the long kiss. Her hand moved to the front of his jeans. Feeling how much he wanted her she moved her fingers to the button but before the button was unfastened, he grabbed her hand. Seth broke the kiss, holding her hand and putting his other hand on her upper arm, he moved his body away from her.

He took a second to catch his breath and shook his head, "We can't do this. Not like this." He was in a panic all of a sudden thinking about all the reasons he shouldn't do what he was about to do. What his body desperately wanted to do more than anything was take her and claim her as his. But she had been drinking, she was upset about her ex showing up, she might go back to D.C., what about what his dad said? And ultimately, they said they would be friends. He couldn't just have a one-night stand with Ophelia Griffin, was that what this would be? Would she want more? He could never leave it alone and just have her once; this was not going to happen.

Ophelia looked at him and moved forward to get rid of the space between them but Seth held her back, "We're friends, right? Just friends."

Ophelia felt foolish. If the alcohol and kissing had not already caused a blush to her cheeks, the embarrassment of him pulling away would have been apparent.

She quickly composed herself, stepping back removing her hand and body from his touch she said, "Right." She gave him a half smile; "I really do have it from here. Thank you for your help tonight." She stepped around him retrieving her t-shirt from her suitcase. She walked to the bathroom speaking over her shoulder, "Will you lock the door on your way out? Good night." She closed the bathroom door and leaned against it letting out the breath she was holding.

Seth stood at the end of her bed running his hand over his face and then fingers through his hair. He couldn't believe what he just did. He stood collecting himself and thought that he didn't know if he was mad that he stopped or mad that he started in the first place. How would they handle what just happened? My God what if it never happens again? Should he wait for her? So much for taking it slow and getting to know each other again. He shook his head and left her bedroom. Seth did what she asked; he locked the front door behind him when he left.

Ophelia woke at 5am with a slight headache but more than that, a badly bruised ego. Christ what was she thinking making out with Seth Corrigan like that? And then he put a stop to it with the "just friends," comment, how humiliating. She willed her body out of bed and went for a long run. When she returned she showered and ate breakfast, feeling more like herself. She had plans to tackle some Christmas shopping and decided to drive to Spanish Fort about 30 minutes away to walk the outdoor mall. She decided she would stay out of downtown Fairhope and any possibility of running into Seth. Around 2pm she received a text message from Seth.

Seth: Checking on you. How are you feeling?

Ophelia rolled her eyes.

Ophelia: Never better. Even went for a morning run. Thanks for checking on me.

Seth: Welcome. Glad to hear you're not hung over. Do you want to talk about last night?

Ophelia hesitated and smirked.

Ophelia: Did we skip out on the bar bill? If we did, I'll drop off the money on my way home this evening.

Seth: No, you paid your bar bill. The waitress thinks you were very generous. Do you want to talk about what happened?

Ophelia: I don't need to talk about what happened with Nick. I was annoyed he showed up but honestly that ship sailed a long time ago. I don't have any unresolved feelings to talk about.

Ophelia gave a little chuckle when she pushed send; she knew Seth wasn't talking about Nick. If she had to text him, she would enjoy herself.

Seth read the text message and wondered if she was messing with him or did she really not care that they almost slept together. He contemplated through his frustration what to send as a response.

Seth: Well that's great. Sounds like you're in a good place.

Ophelia: I am. Thanks for checking on me. You're a good friend.

Seth didn't know how to respond and waited long enough that Ophelia put her phone back in her purse and continued shopping. The chime came in about 15 minutes later.

Seth: I thought you might want to discuss what happened when we got back to the rental. Between you and me.

Ophelia smiled. He couldn't get that out of his mind any more than she could.

Ophelia: No big deal, right? I don't need a discussion if you don't. Like you said last night, just friends. We can blame it on the Grinch shots, we got caught up in the moment. It was dark, and I could have been anyone.

Seth: What the hell is that supposed to mean? You could have been anyone?

Ophelia did feel a little annoyed and why shouldn't she? She was attractive, and he was attracted to her just as much as she was attracted to him. They were grown adults.

Olivia: I'm not the only girl you've ever kissed. Do you normally have discussions the day after you lock lips with a girl? I'm just sayin' it's not like there's something special going on between us, right? Just kissing shared between two friends.

Friend my ass, Seth Corrigan is full of shit, she thought to herself. She watched the dots for a few minutes but didn't receive a message for some time, and then, three words.

Seth: Where are you?

Ophelia: Why?

Seth: Are you angry with me? Can I see you?

Ophelia: I'm not angry. I'm fine. We are fine. I'm Christmas shopping. Have a great day, Friend!

Ophelia decided to get one final blow in.

CHAPTER 5

Shelby drove in from Birmingham arriving at 9pm on December 19th. She put the boys to bed and started helping decorate the Christmas tree.

"Shelby, do you want a glass of red wine?" Mom called from the kitchen.

"Yes, Momma that sounds great." Shelby looked at Seth, "What's wrong with you? Somebody kick your puppy?"

"Nothin' is wrong. I'm fine." Seth continued to hang ornaments on the tree.

Shelby laughed, "Yeah, real convincing. Do you want me to tell you what's wrong?"

Seth looked at Shelby annoyed and walked over to his beer taking a drink, "Please enlighten me, smarty pants."

"You're in love with Ophelia and you're trying to deny it." Shelby didn't look at him, she just kept decorating.

"No, I'm not in love. Why would you say that?" Seth looked at her annoyed.

She turned to look at him, "Let me see, ever since she came back to town, she is all you can talk about. You've always had a thing for her."

Seth looked at her, "I complain about her. It's not like I'm singing her praises."

Shelby laughed, "The last two weeks you have complained about her being too busy to see you, call or text. You have your boxers in a bunch. I haven't talked to her either; she's been busy working. She leaves for Vermont soon with the Attorney General's family. You don't see me pacing the floor in a sour mood."

Seth acted mad, "I'm not pacing the floor. She's toying with me. Who the hell tells someone to have a nice day, FRIEND?" Seth exaggerated the word friend. "Or the latest text, "I'm really tied up, hope you have a great rest of the week, see you at the family Christmas."

Shelby started laughing, "Both nice text messages. Neither one of those are 'eat shit and die'."

Seth looked at her, "Watch your mouth or Momma will give you the soap."

Shelby laughed, "I'm 29 years old. I think Momma knows I say 'shit'. You told her you were just friends. She's being a friend. I don't get to see her or talk to her on the phone all the time. Our text messages are a lot like what you are describing. If you don't want to be friends, you better let her know you want more."

Seth shook his head and took a sip of beer, "You don't know what you are talking about. We are just friends and I'm perfectly fine with that."

Shelby giggled, "Who are you trying to convince? I'm warning you because I love you. If you mess her around and hurt her she will never give you a second chance. You two are the most stubborn people, this is going to be fun to watch."

Mom walked in, "What are you two talking about?"

Shelby took the glass of wine from her mom's hand, "Thank you. Seth is trying to convince himself he's not in love with Ophelia."

Shelby took a sip of wine and walked back to the Christmas tree.

Mom looked at Seth, "Are you in love with Ophelia?"

Seth glared at his sister, "Shelby was dropped on her head when she was a baby and you just never told us."

Mom looked at Seth, "Look at me, Seth." Seth met his mother's eyes. "Are you in love with Ophelia?"

Shelby turned to look at him knowing he would never lie to their mom.

"I don't want to talk about it." Seth took a drink of his beer.

Dad walked in, "What aren't we talking about?"

Mom looked at Dad, "Seth is in love with Ophelia."

Dad shrugged and laughed, "You girls are just now figuring that out? He's wanted that girl since high school."

Seth looked at all of them annoyed, "I'm going home. I'll see my nephews in the morning for breakfast."

Shelby giggled, "Sounds good. Did I mention Ophelia and I are planning on stopping in for the annual Bone and Barrel Christmas party? She got herself packed and ready for her trip so her schedule freed up a little. Looks like I'll get to enjoy your cat and mouse game up close."

Seth looked at Shelby, "There is nothing going on!"

Shelby giggled, "See you tomorrow. Love you big brother!"

The Bone and Barrel Christmas party was out of this world busy with customers packed celebrating the holiday. The staff donned Santa hats and the music the band played had everyone singing along or dancing.

"Holy Shit! This is crazy!" Shelby smiled, talking close to Ophelia's ear so she could hear her.

"No doubt! Great for Seth," Ophelia nodded.

Shelby pointed, "He saved us seats at the bar."

The women headed over to seats mid bar rail. Perfect seating to talk to each other and still be able to watch the band. No sooner than they sat down, two drinks were placed in front of them.

Seth smiled, "Hungry?"

Shelby answered, "Just drinking. Momma fed us before we left the house."

She smiled noticing Seth's eyes on Ophelia. Shelby couldn't blame him. She was gorgeous dressed in a pretty blue cashmere sweater and black dress pants and heels.

Ophelia felt her cheeks blush thinking of the last time she had seen Seth.

She smiled, touching her stomach, "Full. Your Momma made spaghetti. Thank you for the beer."

He nodded, hesitating for a moment before going back to fulfilling customer orders. Ophelia looked beautiful and he wanted to tell her but thought better of it. Did friends tell each other they were beautiful? Good Lord, this was getting complicated.

Ophelia and Shelby laughed, enjoying conversation with several friends from high school, one of which was a prominent attorney in Birmingham. He was home visiting family. Keith Duffy was in Seth's graduating class.

"Ophelia, will you dance with me?" Keith extended his hand to her.

"Sure," Ophelia agreed taking his hand and hopping off her barstool.

Keith led her to the dance floor, turning to her. Seth took notice, watching Ophelia laugh while Keith held her in his arms. Granted they weren't dancing cheek to cheek, but Keith had his arm wrapped around her and was touching her lower back. Ophelia kept a little distance between them so she could carry on the conversation that she found entertaining. He could feel a degree of aggravation and jealousy begin to take over watching her laugh and enjoy whatever Keith was telling her.

Shelby tapped the bar to get Seth's attention, "Friends huh? Maybe you should cut in?"

Seth's eyebrow lifted, "She can dance with whom ever she wants. Keith's a nice guy, made a name for himself in Birmingham."

"Hmmm. Wonder if she likes him?" Shelby looked at Ophelia dancing. The two were definitely talking up a storm. She looked back at her brother, "Whatcha gonna do? Let that happen?"

"Mind your business." Seth walked away.

Ophelia thanked Keith for the dance, excusing herself to walk to the ladies restroom. Before she made it to the lengthy line, she was stopped by a handsome 20-something guy.

"You have gorgeous hair." The guy touched her arm to get her attention.

"Thank you." Ophelia smiled.

"Can I buy you a beer?" The handsome guy smiled.

"I'm on my way to the ladies room," as soon as the words left her mouth Ophelia felt a hand clasp her elbow ushering her towards a door that read "Office".

She looked up at an unhappy Seth.

"Hey, what's wrong?" Ophelia asked but Seth took the few more steps, opening the office door and forcing her entrance. It wasn't exactly a shove but she didn't walk in on her own.

Seth closed the door behind him leaving all the sound on the other side. "What the hell are you doing? The guys that come in here are only looking for one thing."

Ophelia laughed, "I can take care of myself. I know what young guys are looking for. Thanks but I don't need savin'."

She reached for the door handle but Seth placed his hand on hers stopping it from turning. "You're avoiding me."

"I've been busy. The A.G.'s schedule has been big and we have the upcoming travel for the holiday," Ophelia's eyes met his, giving him the answer.

"What is going on with Keith? You know he lives in Birmingham?" Seth added.

The corner of Ophelia's mouth turned up, "Seth Corrigan, you're jealous." She chimed.

Seth stood back crossing his arms over his chest, "I'm looking out for you. I'm not jealous."

"Keith's a nice man. He's done well for himself, has his own law practice in Birmingham. Thanks for looking out for me but I'm not in any danger," Ophelia smirked.

They were both silent for a few minutes.

"Is that all you wanted to say? Seems like a big ta do bringing me to your office to warn me that Keith lives in Birmingham," Ophelia waited feeling a little cocky.

Seth stared at Ophelia's lips, nodding yes.

"You're sure?" Ophelia bit her lower lip on purpose knowing what his eyes were focusing on.

Seth's hands grabbed the sides of her face suddenly while his lips crashed against hers. He pushed her back against the door, pressing his body against hers. The kiss was intense, putting Ophelia's head in a spin. She held his waist with both hands to keep standing with wobbly knees. The kiss was causing havoc with her entire body; she felt the jolt of electricity in every nerve.

Just when she thought the kiss was over and she could catch her breath, Seth's tongue licked her lower lip diving back in her mouth. His hands slid down her shoulders allowing Ophelia's hands to move up with her arms wrapping around his neck, her fingers touching the thick wavy hair he kept short.

Seth wrapped his arms around her waist, lifting her slightly and moving her to his desk. Ophelia felt the top of his desk press against the back of her legs. Seth broke the kiss on her lips only to run his tongue and lips down her neck. His hands moved quickly under her sweater, touching the lace of her bra.

"Christ, you're so fucking beautiful. Your skin is so soft." Seth kissed from her collarbone back to her lips.

Ophelia arched towards him, her breasts and nipples longing for his touch, his mouth, his attention. Soft sounds escaped her when his fingers kneaded her nipple through the fabric of her bra. His other hand held her lower back under her sweater touching her skin with his fingertips tickling gently before holding her firm against his body.

When his lips left hers to kiss her chin, she whispered, "Your hands feel good." She moved her lips to kiss his neck, moving his shirt collar away from his neck. Seth's head fell back slightly, enjoying her wet kiss on his skin. The back of his hand gently moved down her abdomen to the button of her pants.

Ophelia's voice was sweet on his neck, "Are we just friends? Is that all you want?"

Seth's mind went from wanting and needing to touch and kiss every inch of Ophelia, to complete panic. He stopped moving. She stopped and waited for him to answer her question, to move his hands or to breathe, but he was frozen. Like a dear in headlights frozen. Ophelia backed up slightly, moving to the side away from his desk to straighten her sweater. She smoothed her hair back into place, righting all that he had wronged with her appearance. She looked at him hoping for something but he only looked at her with uncertainty.

Her lips curled into a small smile, "Thanks for looking out for me but I'm good at reading people. No need to worry about me when it comes to men, I can handle myself."

She walked out of the office closing the door behind her. Ophelia figured he needed a couple minutes to calm the extreme bulge in his jeans. She waited her turn for the ladies bathroom then returned to Shelby.

Shelby was chatting with several high school friends when Ophelia returned, Keith hot on her trail to talk to her. The conversation continued with more courtroom stories. Ophelia thought it was a little comical that Seth was bent out of shape, if he only knew Keith was more interested in talking about his courtroom prowess than anything romantic. Keith was interested in Keith. Ophelia had no doubt that any woman would be just an add-on to Keith's self-proclaimed incredible life. She wanted more, to be someone's everything. She wanted Seth if she was being honest with herself.

"Dance with me," Seth whispered in her ear approaching her from behind.

He took her waist in his hands, steering her to an open place on the dance floor. Ophelia said nothing but let Seth move her to the dance floor. She turned to dance with him, her eyes meeting his. Seth took her hand and her waist in his hands swaying their bodies to the music. He pressed her body to his, leaving no space between them. Seth hoped Keith took notice.

"I, we are friends. I mean isn't that what we said?" Seth spoke in her ear.

Ophelia sighed with a slight nod, "That's what we said."

"I have no right to be jealous but I don't want you talking to Keith." Seth paused, "I don't know, I'm trying to do the right thing.

Be your friend." His mouth grazed her forehead.

Ophelia lifted an eyebrow, "The right thing for who? A better question is, how do you feel about me, Seth?"

Seth pulled her a little closer, staying silent while they completed their dance.

CHAPTER 6

Christmas Eve Dinner at the Corrigan's was at 4pm but Shelby and Ophelia couldn't wait that long to see each other. Ophelia knocked on the door at 11am wearing a pretty green dress. Shelby opened her parent's front door and the two hugged each other tight.

"This is the first Christmas in forever that we are in the same city. I'm so excited. Come up to my room while I get ready. Daddy took the boys fishing on the dock so it's just us." Shelby led the way to her childhood bedroom. "Tell me everything that is going on," Shelby insisted.

"I just talked to you on the phone last night, you know pretty much everything," Ophelia smiled and shrugged. She had worked the previous four days.

"Really? We confirmed our plans for today. We haven't really talked since the Christmas party and you didn't spill what was going on between you and my brother," Shelby said, pursing her lips.

Ophelia paused, thinking if she wanted to talk about Seth and decided against it. "I'm going to move to the bay house when I get back in town and start going through my parents things," Ophelia half smiled.

"That's good. Do you want me to come help?" Shelby offered.

"Thank you for the offer but I want to do it myself," Ophelia didn't exactly smile but wasn't upset either.

Shelby nodded, "Tell me what is going on with you and my brother." Shelby turned looking at her, "I did notice the subject change. You're not getting off that easy."

"I have no idea what you mean. Seth and I are friends." Ophelia said convincingly.

"Bullshit," Shelby pointed at her, "Don't you dare use your FBI mind games. Tell me the truth."

Ophelia laughed and shrugged, "Your mouth is not very lady like for Christmas Eve." Ophelia tried again to deflect but Shelby continued the glare. "Ok. I really have no idea. He wants to be friends. I'm being friends." She quoted with her fingers in the air when she said she was being friends.

Shelby laughed, "You two are the most stubborn people I know. Do you want to be just friends?"

"It's not that simple. You're brother is a ladies man. He's got girls lined up at the bar hoping for a chance to go out with him. I'm not that kind of girl. I doubt he's ready to give that up and I'm not going to be one of his groupies. Plus he's busy convincing himself he doesn't have feelings for me, so I suspect he will talk himself right out of anything more than the friendship he's convincing everyone we have," Ophelia explained with a smirk.

Shelby laughed, "This is going to be great. You both are going to torture each other. Has he kissed you?"

"I'm not trying to torture him. What are we 13? We are grown adults I don't think we ask things like that anymore."

Shelby laughed, "He has. Holy shit. That's why he's freaking out." She clapped her hands together then rubbed them like she was plotting something good, "I'm going to have so much fun teasing him!"

"Shelby you are twisted. I think you are enjoying this a little too much." Ophelia shook her head.

Shelby smiled with a thoughtful look, "Ophelia, I love you. Please be careful with my brother's heart. Seth is scared of taking a chance, especially if he might get hurt; he would never admit that. Letting the girls in the bar flirt with him is safe because he's not risking his heart. I know for a fact since you moved back, he hasn't been on a date." She raised an eyebrow, "I've already warned him that if he hurts you, I'll kill him. I don't want to see either of you broken hearted."

Ophelia smiled, "You don't have anything to worry about. I don't think your brother is ever going to act on whatever feelings he has. I'm sure he'll be back on the dating scene soon."

It was 3:30pm when Ophelia snuggled with Shelby's two little boys, Jake, aged four, and Owen, aged five on the family room couch. They were getting a little pre-dinner reading of *How the Grinch Stole Christmas* in before everyone was called to the table. While Ophelia read she was interrupted several times with questions.

"Why is the Grinch green?" Jake asked.

"He is jealous and jealous people turn green," Ophelia smiled about her explanation.

"Why do you have red hair?" Owen asked.

"I ate a bunch of strawberries when I was little and my hair turned red," Ophelia smiled.

"Why don't you have kids?" Owen asked.

Ophelia smiled, "Did you get a job at the FBI? Because you sure do ask a lot of questions." She tickled Owen.

"Do you like kids?" Jake asked.

"Yes, I love kids. I ordered a couple from the stork; they just haven't arrived yet. It takes a good while to get the delivery," Ophelia smiled.

"Aunt Ophelia, we want you to stay in Alabama," Owen said pressing his sweet face to her chest.

"Hmm. Did your Momma put you up to that?" She stroked his hair.

Jake giggled, "No, Uncle Seth."

Owen was quick to say looking up at her, "Uncle Seth said you love the ocean like we do."

"I do love the ocean but I love the two of you more. Give me kisses."

Both boys attacked her squeezing her around the neck and peppering her with kisses.

"What is going on in here?" Seth said standing at the entranceway to the family room. He had been listening to the entire interrogation and Ophelia's funny answers.

Both boys screamed, "Uncle Seth." They leaped off the couch and ran to him.

The boys hugged his legs almost knocking him over. He patted their backs looking at Ophelia. Ophelia stood up, straightening her dress and hair that was messed up from the boys attacking her. She was nervous to see Seth; they hadn't run into each other since the Christmas party.

Ophelia spoke first, "Hi Seth, Merry Christmas."

He smiled at her, "Merry Christmas. You look pretty in green."

"Thank you. You look handsome."

"Aunt Ophelia was reading the Grinch. Do you want her to read it to you?" Jake asked Seth.

Seth laughed, "I don't think she was actually reading the Grinch, you ask too many questions. You have to listen when she reads and not talk."

Owen said, "But she has all the answers. She likes to read to us like that." Owen waited for just a second saying, "Uncle Seth did you order kids from the stork? You don't have any and that's what Aunt Ophelia did. She's getting some, you should too."

Ophelia smiled putting her hand over her mouth.

"I'm not sure how to order kids. I'll have to ask Aunt Ophelia how she did that." Seth raised an eyebrow and looked at Ophelia.

Ophelia's face was full of mischief and she smiled.

After dinner everyone sat around the Christmas tree watching the boys open their Christmas presents.

Shelby spoke up, "What do you say? Give hugs and kisses to everyone."

The boys walked to each person giving hugs, kisses and saying thank you.

Owen sat next to Ophelia, "I love you, Aunt Ophelia."

Ophelia pulled him to her lap kissing and hugging him, "I love you, little man."

She looked at Shelby and gave her a smile that let her know how sweet her son was.

Shelby smiled, "The boys are crazy about you."

"I'm crazy about them." Ophelia nodded.

"They told me that they are no longer going to eat strawberries, any idea why they would say that?" Shelby looked at Ophelia.

Ophelia looked at Shelby trying to convey shock, "No idea."

"Because they turn your hair red," Jake laughed.

The whole family started laughing.

Through giggles, Ophelia looked at Mom and Dad Corrigan, "I have something for you."

Mom Corrigan said, "You know better than to do that."

"I know but I didn't buy this," Ophelia handed Mom Corrigan an envelope.

Mom opened it, pulling out two tickets to the Striper's Mardi Gras Ball and paid reservations for a hotel the night of the ball.

"The Sipes Family have been Striper's for years. When was the last time you two went to a Mardi Gras Ball? Do you want to go?" Ophelia smiled.

Mom Corrigan's eyes were wide, "It's been years. Yes I want to go. Are you going?"

Ophelia nodded, "I am. I'll be working but I'll be there."

Seth spoke up, "Do you get to wear a ball gown or do you have to go in a business suit?"

"I'll wear a ball gown." Ophelia answered.

Seth looked at her, "What about your gun? You don't carry at the ball?"

Ophelia smiled, "I always carry when I'm working."

"How do you manage that in a ball gown?" Seth was curious.

"I'll manage," Ophelia avoided specifics figuring he didn't really want to know.

Seth gestured for her to continue, "How?"

Ophelia looked at him, "Thigh holster. My ball gown has a slit from the ankle to above the knee."

Shelby laughed out loud, "Ponder that for a while Seth." She laughed again, "Who is ready for dessert?" She patted her brother's shoulder when she stood to take the boys to the kitchen.

Ophelia stood up and followed the group to the kitchen leaving Seth to deal with his thoughts on her gun carrying.

It was 10'oclock; the little boys had been a sleep for a couple hours with the adults enjoying drinks. It was time for Ophelia to say good-bye. She was flying out at 6am with the Attorney General's detail. Ophelia said good-bye to Mom and Dad Corrigan first, following up with Shelby and Seth in the kitchen finishing their beers.

Ophelia hugged Shelby, "I'm sorry I'm going to miss Michael. Tell your wonderful husband Merry Christmas for me. I love you. I'll call you after Christmas."

Shelby hugged her a little longer, "Love you. Don't break a leg skiing. Can you come to Birmingham soon?"

"I'm not skiing. Let me see what I can get worked out, I'll try to get a long weekend off." Ophelia stepped back and looked at Seth. She moved close to him and hugged him, "Merry Christmas. I'll see you when I get back."

Seth hugged her tight, "Merry Christmas."

CHAPTER 7

Six weeks went by quickly with Ophelia keeping up with the Attorney General and his family's schedule. Work was very good with minimal travel giving her plenty of time to accomplish projects at the Bay House. She hired contractors to paint the house and upgrade the docks. With only a few cold winter days, all of the work was getting completed quickly. The inside painting and remodeling on the downstairs living room and kitchen was moving along. She was happy with the paint colors, new furniture and window dressings, along with the updates she made to the downstairs guest bedroom. Ophelia was utilizing the guest bedroom as her bedroom until the upstairs was redone.

She managed a visit to Birmingham for three days in late January to see Shelby, Michael and the boys. She limited Seth's access to her when she returned from her work travel over Christmas. Ophelia had a hard time not wanting more than friendship and Seth had yet to make a move that wasn't more than flirting or inviting her to hang out as friends. She could tell he was aggravated with her during their conversations or text message exchanges because she wouldn't make time to spend with him.

"Your brother sent beautiful pink roses to me for Valentine's Day. They were waiting for me when I got home tonight," Ophelia called Shelby, giving her the latest.

"Now if he would ask you out on a date, he could stop complaining about missing you," Shelby commented with sarcasm.

Ophelia had kept Shelby appraised of the requests to hang out or meet up that Seth sent Ophelia. He wanted to date her without actually dating her and Shelby knew Ophelia wasn't going to do it. Ophelia made it a rule to only see Seth when it involved their group of friends.

"He's not missing me that much. I stopped in the bar with my co-workers last week and he sat down with us for a little while," Ophelia offered.

"I know. He complained that the only time you go to the bar is with people. He's not happy he can't get you alone. Sunday dinner at Mom and Dad's and friends all around is making Seth disgruntled," she laughed.

Ophelia shrugged, "I don't know what to tell him. I don't hang out with any male friends and Seth is dangerous for me. I'm not going to feel something he's not. He'll have to live with it. Michelle's husband is playing tomorrow night so I'm meeting her up there."

"Does Seth know?" Shelby asked.

"Yes. I called to thank him for the roses. He asked if I wanted to meet for a drink or dessert tonight but I got home late and said I would see him tomorrow at the bar."

Shelby laughed, "Oh Lord, he'll be calling me."

"Sorry, but Seth wants to be friends and I need to have boundaries so I don't let myself want anything more," Ophelia explained.

"I understand. Owen is asking for a glass of water. He doesn't like water until he's in the bed for the night," Shelby laughed. "Have a good night."

Shelby received a call before she walked upstairs to bed. She answered, "Hello big brother. Happy Valentine's Day."

"Happy Valentine's Day. What did you and Mike do?" Seth asked.

"He bought me flowers, candy and took me to an early dinner since it's a school night. He's dealing with the boys right now. They have been up hungry, thirsty and needing to use the bathroom about five times."

Seth laughed, "Good luck getting them up in the morning."

"I know right, luckily it's kindergarten and pre-k. So why are you calling me? I figured you would be out on a hot date," Shelby said pushing the envelope.

"Nobody I wanted to take out. I'm busy with the bar," Seth responded.

"I heard you sent Ophelia roses in her favorite color. Pull the trigger and ask her out on a date. You know you want to," Shelby sighed.

"Did she like the roses? I mean she thanked me said they were beautiful but when I asked her to meet me for a drink she said she couldn't." Seth paused, "She's avoiding me. I mean I see her but only because we are both included in something. I've been asking to help with the bay house or meet her for drinks. I want to catch up with her but she won't see me."

"Ask her out on a date. Stop with this meet up or hang out B.S. Call it what it is. You want to date her, spend time with just her. Stop it with the just friends thing; you're not fooling anyone. The only thing you are managing to do is make yourself miserable."

Seth sighed, "And if it doesn't work out? You know she's undecided about staying in Fairhope. Ophelia doesn't know what she wants to do about the FBI once this detail is over. What if she decides to leave?"

"That's what this is about? Seth, we never know what our future holds. She is updating the bay house and making it her own. You're right, she doesn't know what the next assignment will be but don't you think if she was in a relationship she would make that decision with someone?" Shelby waited a few moments and continued, "If you are looking for a no risk situation when it comes to love, you'll never find one."

Seth considered what she said but didn't comment. "I'll let you get back to Mike. Happy Valentine's Day. Love you."

"Love you. She loved the roses. Call her and ask her out on a real date. Good night." Shelby disconnected the call.

Ophelia took a sip of her wine before answering Michelle, "Valentine's Day was fine. I worked until 9 last night for the A.G. to take Mrs. Sipes to dinner. I did get several Valentines." Ophelia smiled, "Homemade. Shelby's boys and the A.G.'s girls made cute Valentines for me. I always laugh when a child draws a picture of me, I have bright orange hair," she giggled.

Seth smiled listening to the girl's conversation instead of the one the men at the table were having. Ophelia's hair was a beautiful shade of red but he noticed his nephews always colored Ophelia's hair either bright red or bright orange in their pictures.

"Come on. What about a grown up romance?" Michelle asked.

Seth listened closer.

"Who has time? I'm busy." Ophelia sat back taking another sip of her wine.

"Nobody at work?" Michelle asked.

Ophelia shook her head, "Nope. Let's talk about your love life. Ken is touring, are you going with him?"

"Just part of the tour. Most of the venues he's working are a day trip so he'll be coming home most nights."

Ophelia nodded, "He sounds great. You have to be so proud of him."

"I am." Michelle looked at her husband starry eyed.

Seth leaned towards Ophelia, "So, what are your weekend plans?"

"Saturday morning fire arms training. Sunday dinner at your parents. Other than that, I'm working on the bay house." Ophelia sipped her wine.

"Need some help?" Seth offered.

Ophelia shook her head with a laugh, "Trust me, you don't want to deal with the contractors or me. I'm a little more precise than they want me to be."

Seth was again disappointed, "Dance with me." He stood up taking her hand not giving her an option to say no. Seth walked Ophelia to the dance floor and turning towards her he pulled her body to his. He swayed with her for a few minutes before whispering, "I'm going to spin you, ready?"

She smiled with a nod. Ophelia spun out under the arm he lifted that was holding her hand. She came back to his arms with a smile and said, "Your mom."

Seth nodded, "You bet. I had to know how to dance with a girl. I was popular at Prom," He winked sending her off again to spin but this time he doubled up.

Ophelia smiled big again, returning to his arms, "I can see why all the girls swooned. You're really good."

"Thank you. We should do this more often," Seth offered.

Ophelia didn't respond other than moving her face closer to his shoulder. When the song ended they both clapped their hands for Ken and his band while walking back to the table. Ophelia sat down next to Michelle who was talking to a girl she recognized from school but didn't know.

"Ophelia, this is Kaitlyn Lane," Michele introduced the newcomer.

"Hi. Pleasure to meet you," Ophelia offered her hand to shake.

Kaitlyn returned the hello and shook Ophelia's hand, "I was two years after you in school. Your Momma was my favorite teacher."

"Thank you." Ophelia smiled.

Kaitlyn's eyes diverted to Seth who took a seat next to Ophelia. "Hey Seth, good to see you."

"Hey Kaitlyn, how have you been?" Seth smiled taking a drink of his beer.

"I'm good. I was hoping we could get together for dinner this week? I owe you a home cooked meal. I know it's been awhile since I made that offer; it's about time you collected. I've been busy adjusting to a new grade this year. I'm teaching 8th. It's a bit more challenging than 3rd." Kaitlyn's eyes lit up with a small laugh.

Seth ignored the dinner invitation, "I'm sure it is, 8th graders start putting their teachers to the test."

"That they do. Do you have the same school schedule at the college this semester?" Kaitlyn asked.

Seth was very aware that Ophelia was paying attention. He feared it was blatantly obvious he had dated Kaitlyn with her knowing his school schedule.

"I'm working Monday, Wednesday and Friday." Seth watched Ophelia comment something to Michelle and leave the table.

He spotted Ophelia standing at the bar talking to a group he recognized from high school. It was the same group she and Shelby talked to at the Christmas party minus Keith. He wondered if she didn't return to the table because of Kaitlyn.

When he found a break in the conversation he stood, "I'm going to check on the staff. Anyone need anything?"

The table responded with a couple orders, which Seth had their waitress take to the table. He checked in with the bartender but kept his eye on Ophelia. When she placed her empty beer bottle on the bar he opened two beers and walked around joining her.

Seth handed Ophelia one of the bottles, "Come with me. I need to talk to you."

He took her by her free hand until they reached the office door. Seth let her hand go to open the door, letting her walk in first. Ophelia walked in, not sure where to stand or exactly what he wanted to talk about. She walked to his desk and leaned her bottom against it, waiting for him to say something. Seth strolled over, leaning against the desk right next to her, so close their hips touched.

"Let's catch up. It hasn't been a you and me conversation in a long time."

Ophelia shrugged, "I think you know everything. I'm just working and when I'm not working the bay house is keeping me busy. How's your school semester going?"

"Good. I'm instructing two different courses three days a week. I have second or third year students." Seth took a drink of his beer, "Have you given thought to what you want to do after your assignment ends with the A.G.?"

Ophelia shook her head, "No. I won't be reassigned until the end of this year. I'm still getting situated here, I've been to the field office several times; it's too early to have a conversation about what comes next with the FBI. Plus, I'm trying to make the bay house mine, I get to see my Momma whenever I want so I'm not ready to think about what comes next career wise."

Seth nodded. "I'm not having dinner with Kaitlyn."

Ophelia stiffened, "That's not my business. You can have dinner with anyone you like." Ophelia stood up straight, "I think we are all caught up."

"Hold on," Seth stood placing his beer bottle on the desk. "I took Kaitlyn out a couple times last fall. No big deal. It was just lunch."

"You don't owe me an explanation. I know you date. You should. We are just friends so by all means have at it." Ophelia was annoyed he brought her in his office for this. When she stepped forward he stepped in front of her.

"Have at it?" He frowned, "Phe, I…" Seth paused, looking in her eyes long enough that he couldn't remember what exactly he was going to say.

His face bent slowly towards hers, hoping she would offer her lips to him.

Ophelia tilted her face up, "Seth…" His lips took hers in a soft, gentle kiss that was the first in an encore of kisses that produced more and more heat. Ophelia pulled her face away. "Friends don't kiss like that." She shook her head trying to clear it, "Friends don't kiss."

Seth didn't respond, he planted his lips back on hers, stopping her from talking. He wrapped his arms around her, edging her body back to the desk to lean against. His kisses were no longer gentle but full of need. Seth's teeth tugged at her lower lip then he took his time nibbling from one side of her mouth to the other. He added light suction to her lower lip before his tongue pushed to explore her tongue. They were both winded when his lips let up only to explore down her neck. His hands held her tight with hers doing the same to him.

"I miss you. I don't know your body but God I miss it." Seth's voice was labored kissing down her neck, pushing her back slightly to kiss the cleavage that was exposed. The feel of Ophelia's fingers tugging his hair slightly excited him all the more. His mouth moved upward, conquering her neck and chin before crashing back on her lips. Seth's hands roamed her body exploring her shape over her clothes. When his finger sought out the button on her pants Ophelia's hand gently held his in place, not allowing him to continue. Ophelia took her lips away from his to speak.

She let her breathing steady for a second and opened her eyes to look into his, "I want you to touch me, I want you, Seth. I know how I feel and what I want. Do you?"

Seth looked at her. Of course he knew how he felt and it was obvious how much he wanted her but this was not the way to have her for the first time. His office, no way. He wouldn't just date this woman; Ophelia was it for him, the one. He was afraid, nervous, not exactly sure. Seth took her hand in his dropping them to his side away from the button on her pants.

"I want us to spend time together," slipped out of his mouth. *Fuck was that really what he was going to offer as an answer.*

Ophelia moved away from him straightening herself so she didn't look messed around. Her back was to him, she refused to look at him out of embarrassment and anger.

"Don't kiss me again, Seth. Friends do not kiss. Don't bring me in your office, don't…" She caught her breath, "Just don't." She stormed out of the office, slamming the door behind her.

Seth stood in his office running his hand over his face and through his hair. He knew that was a colossal fuck up. He pushed himself up from the top of his desk knowing he needed to face the music and apologize. Seth walked back to the table of friends finding Ophelia gone. He looked at his phone contemplating exactly what text message to send.

Seth: I'm sorry. That was not what I meant exactly. I mean I want to spend time together, of course. Do I really need to declare my intentions, can't you just go easy on me? Let me see you.

Seth thought that was a good text, of course it was. She should be more understanding; just because she knows her feelings, doesn't mean he does. He's a guy; guys don't know their feelings. He shook his head wondering if he could retract the text message because that was a cop out and he did know exactly how he felt. He was in love with Ophelia. "God Damnit," Seth looked around, realizing he said the curse out loud.

The dots appeared and he waited for her response.

Ophelia sat in her driveway contemplating what to say. She was so angry not only with him, but with herself. Christ, she would have stripped naked in his office. No more games. She was not going to make a big deal of it, she was just going to stay away from Seth which is what she intended from the first time she walked in his bar.

Ophelia: I'll see you at Sunday dinner at your parents. No harm no foul. Let's just forget tonight every happened. Have a good night.

Seth read the text message thinking, *what the fuck?* He was furious. What was that supposed to mean, no harm no foul? How could she be so, so, unaffected? She could just forget about it?

Seth: I'm not sure what that means, neither of us will forget about it. I am truly sorry I said what I did. I would like a chance to talk face to face. Can I come over?

Ophelia took no time at all to respond.

Ophelia: You have got to be joking. You do not get to see me again without a chaperone. Go find some other girl you can toy with. If you show up at my door, I will call a cop. Better yet I'll arrest you my damn self for trespassing. Stay away from me!

Seth's eyes widened reading her response. She was pissed. Not a little pissed, full on redhead furious.

Seth: I'll see you Sunday and we'll talk about this. Again, I'm sorry. I said the wrong thing.

Seth knew he would need to send flowers, and maybe some sort of jewelry. That meant calling Shelby. He sighed as he walked behind the bar to help wait on customers.

Ophelia listened to Shelby laughing hysterically on the other end of the phone. "I'm hanging up. Stop laughing!" Ophelia was furious.

"He really did think you would have him arrested. He called at 8 am this morning and asked if you had shared what happened last night," Shelby continued to snicker.

"Your brother is an ass hat thinking I was going to let him come over to talk. Seriously? That man is not getting anywhere near me," Ophelia huffed.

Shelby tried to compose herself, "You don't mean that. He's a man and a chicken shit. You scare him, not because of the arrest threat but because he knows exactly how he feels and its nothing he's felt before. Be pissed but forgive him eventually."

"No, no way. I'm going to meet some nice man and date him. There are nice men out there and I'm going to find one. Seth can keep to what he does best, date the customers that come in his bar, the ones that throw themselves at him." Ophelia pulled in a parking spot at the gun range.

"You don't mean that. Are you at the gun range?" Shelby asked knowing where Ophelia was driving.

"Yes, I just parked," Ophelia admitted.

"Go shoot something. You'll feel better," Shelby laughed, "call me after dinner on Sunday; I can't wait to hear what happens."

CHAPTER 8

"She didn't come to dinner. Instead she made beignets and brought them to Mom and Dad this morning. She made some excuse about work and was long gone before I arrived. Ophelia is a pain in the ass. She's going to avoid me even more than she already does," Seth called Shelby Sunday after dinner.

"What do you expect?" She told you she wanted you and you were like 'uh, uh I want to spend time with you?'" Shelby made a stupid voice when she quoted what Seth said. "Talk about choking. Good luck, dude. Maybe you should have taken your sister's advice and asked her out on a real date? Or better yet, tell her you love her, you want her; in your words declare your intentions. I might agree that you are an ass hat!" Shelby smirked.

"What? She called me an ass hat?" Seth ignored everything else that was said.

"Of course that's what you heard. Are you serious? Seth, you are acting like a dumb ass. Go after her with serious intentions or you are going to lose her. Did you send her flowers?"

"No, I brought them to dinner." Seth stated.

Shelby sighed, "It's been two days since you screwed up, you should have done something yesterday. Now it looks like you did nothing. Good Lord, I've been married for 8 years and know more about dating than you do!"

"Give me a break. You and Mike have been together since the 9th grade. I hardly think you can compare dating in your 30's to what you have going on," Seth said with annoyance.

"Mike still dates me. He brings flowers for no reason or sends them when he hurts my feelings. We still do things to make each other feel special and to let each other know that the other comes first. That's not different than what you should be doing. Get your shit together, you're wasting time."

CHAPTER 9

Four FBI Agents walked in to Bone and Barrel on St. Patrick's Day dressed in casual clothes, Ophelia was one of the four. She was dressed in a green long sleeve t-shirt that said, "Irish Every Day". She flanked right, walking away from the bar watching the A.G. and Mrs. Sipes who wanted to celebrate the holiday with green beer. Ophelia suggested the Irish Pub but with the outdoor tent it was too out of control for three agents. The A.G. liked Bone and Barrel and even though the crowd was large and the Irish Band loud, it was controllable. Ophelia noticed Seth behind the bar but never made eye contact. She had ignored his requests to stop in to see him at the bar since the Valentine's Day office incident. The only time they had been together was for Sunday dinner at his parents. Talking to him at dinner was fine and things had returned to as normal as possible between them. She smiled and said hello to her friends, but they quickly realized she was working and left her alone to do her job.

Later that night, Seth called Ophelia asking her to come out for a drink. "It's late. Is Michelle and everyone still there?"

"I'm here. Come and spend time with me." Seth demanded with a slur in his voice.

"Maybe you should call it a night? Do you need a ride home?" Ophelia offered.

Seth was very tipsy, "Will you drive me home?"

"Of course. I'll be there in a few minutes." Ophelia drove to the bar, parking out front. She walked in seeing Seth sitting on a barstool like a customer talking to the bartender. She sat down next to him, "Are you ready to go?"

"Yes. Everyone kept buying me shots tonight and I think I had like 12." He gave her a tired smile.

She smiled back, "Water and Advil, you'll be good as new."

They walked to her car. She opened the passenger door, Seth got in and she walked around, getting in the driver's seat.

He was quiet for most of the drive then he asked, "Why don't you like me anymore? I screwed up. I know I did. I said I was sorry."

"What are you talking about? I told you a few weeks ago I wasn't mad. Everything is fine between us." Ophelia answered.

"No it's not. You won't spend any time with me. I've asked to run with you, help you with the house, take you anywhere you want to go and you still you won't let me anywhere near you. What about the flowers? Didn't the flowers help apologize?"

Ophelia pulled up in his driveway. "Where are your keys?"

He pulled them out of his pocket and handed them to her. They both got out of the car and she led him up the small walk to his front door. She unlocked and opened his door.

"Where's your Advil?" She asked entering his house.

"Medicine cabinet."

Seth was sitting on the couch in the living room when Ophelia brought him water and Advil. He took two Advil and drank some of the water.

"You're not going to answer me?" Seth looked at her.

Ophelia sat on the coffee table across from Seth and looked in his eyes, "Do you like me?"

Seth looked at her confused.

"I mean really like me. Not as your friend. How do you feel about me?" Ophelia asked him.

Seth shifted on the couch, he was uncomfortable, not wanting to answer her question.

Ophelia leaned to him and brushed her lips against his. Her voice was sweet, "Good night." She gave him a loving look before she stood. Ophelia left, locking the front door behind her.

It was mid April and the weather on Mobile Bay was in the 80's. Michelle organized a Saturday boat outing, inviting friends to spend the day on Magnolia River tying up at a sandbar. The water was cold but the sun was hot and it was easy to stand calf deep in the water to drink a few beers and socialize.

Ophelia was about an hour behind everyone since she worked that morning. The A.G.'s daughters had a ballet recital so she escorted the A.G., Mrs. Sipes and the girls to the event. She arrived at the sandbar at around 2:30pm. Ken, Michelle's husband, and Seth helped secure Ophelia's boat when she pulled up. It was the first time she had seen Seth since St. Patrick's Day. It seemed that the two had missed each other at family dinner with one or the other being unavailable.

Ophelia took her tank top off, grabbed a beer and stood in her bikini on the sand talking to Michelle. Seth barely spoke to her when she arrived. He decided to walk over to a different group of friends since it felt too difficult for him to look at her and not want to touch her.

The sandbar was full of people, some strangers and some friends of friends. Ophelia was introduced to several people, a few being men that she had never met before. Seth wasn't in her immediate proximity but managed to keep a close eye on who was talking to her and how she was acting with them. After a few hours people were starting to leave and one of the men asked Ophelia for her phone number.

"I'm sorry I'm interested in someone. But it was really nice to meet you," Ophelia politely denied the request.

Ophelia decided it was time to say her good-byes but didn't bother looking Seth's way. She untied the boat and asked Ken to push her off. She drove her boat home and had it on the lift when Seth pulled up. He tied up to her guest dock and got off his boat, walking towards her. She was pulling her bag off the boat and found her tank top, putting it on over her bikini as he approached. She could see Seth was mad and when he spoke he sounded frustrated like a child not getting his way.

"I'm sick and tired of you barely talking to me. You say hi and bye. You could have called or texted that you were coming today. It's been almost a month and you haven't stopped in the bar one time."

Ophelia had a small smile and shook her head, "I asked you a question and you never answered me. You haven't called or texted me in the last month. You didn't tell me you were going to Magnolia River today. I'm sick and tired of you dancing around what is completely obvious." Ophelia walked to him, lifted up on her toes and wrapped her arms around his neck. Her mouth was soft and loving on his. She kissed him breathless. Seth's hands held her lower back; his grip tight.

She lowered to her feet, lifted her face to look him in the eyes, "You need to decide how you feel because you can't have it both ways. You either want to be with me or we are friends. Friends don't talk every day, they take a backseat to work and me finding someone else." She took his hand and turned, leading him to his boat. She untied one of the ropes and handed it to him. She walked over to the other rope, "Get on your boat."

Seth, still in a daze from the kiss and what she said, got on his boat. She untied the other rope and pushed his boat away from the dock, "Go home and get your head and heart figured out."

It was nearly 8pm when Ophelia heard footsteps coming up the stairs to the back deck. She was sitting outside reading the latest American Bar Association Journal. The weather was still nice, and she was comfortable wearing jeans and a t-shirt. She had sweet tea in her hand and looked up when Seth stood at the top of the steps.

He smiled, "Hi. I brought tacos from Dragonfly."

"Mmm. Sounds good. I don't have very many groceries," she grinned, "come on in."

Ophelia stood, taking the journal and her tea. She opened the sliding glass door and walked to the kitchen. Seth followed, looking around. She had been busy.

He put the take-out bag on the counter.

"Would you like sweet tea, water or beer?" Ophelia opened the refrigerator.

"Tea," Seth said. He was so nervous, managing one-word answers was about all he could handle for the moment.

Ophelia looked at him, he looked terrified. She poured his tea, "Do you want to eat or can I show you what I've done to the house?"

"Show me the house." He wasn't really hungry; he just wanted to bring the food as an additional reason to come to see her.

Ophelia talked about the color in the kitchen and the new pantry. She walked him to the living room and showed him the windows had been replaced and the new paint and window dressings.

"I had all the trim painted after I painted the walls. Do you like it?"

"It's beautiful," Seth smiled. He could see she was happy.

"The furniture is new. I probably need more – it looks a little empty but I'm not sure what to add. I was thinking about a large bookcase. I have all my law books and thought that would look nice."

Seth nodded, "I think that would look fine. You could put your shell collection on the shelf," he smiled.

Ophelia laughed, "That might just fit on the shelf. Momma made me downsize when I filled up my bedroom."

"What about the upstairs?" Seth asked.

Ophelia shook her head. "I have the guest bedroom and the bathrooms done down here so I've been living down here. The upstairs is harder for me. I've been trying to box up their bedroom but I can't get through it."

"Why don't you let my Mom or Shelby help you? Or I will help you?"

Ophelia smiled, "Maybe I will." She changed the subject, "So do you think the neutral color is too boring?"

Seth smiled shaking his head; "No I think it looks warm and inviting. Plus you have enough color with the pillows and drapes."

Ophelia smiled, putting her hands on her hips looking around, "That's what I thought too. Did you notice I had the house painted and docks rebuilt? I decided to use some of my trust fund money to get all the updates done."

"Your parents would like what you've done with it. It looks like you," Seth said as he continued to look around.

Ophelia looked at him and wondered what he was going to say to her. She walked back in the kitchen island and picked up her tea, taking a drink. Seth did the same. She decided she wasn't going to say anything else; she turned and looked at him. When Seth's eyes met hers he moved quickly, taking her face in his hands and letting his lips take over hers. She responded by grasping the sides of his shirt in her fingers. Seth thoroughly kissed her then took a break, resting his forehead to hers.

"I have it figured out. I'm sorry. I knew what I wanted all along I was just nervous and…" he paused.

Ophelia smiled, "I'm scared too. I want to be with you. I don't want to be just your friend."

Ophelia found his lips firm and needing her. They kissed each other unable to hold back their hands from wandering over each other's clothes.

It was Ophelia who backed up, her heart was racing and she was trying to catch her breath. "Maybe we should eat the food you brought," she smiled, almost laughing at how breathless she was.

"I don't want the food I brought." Seth walked after her, "I came here for you."

She giggled, "You're looking at me like I'm your dinner." She backed up, putting her hand out and keeping him away. She continued to laugh, watching him coming for her.

Seth grabbed the wrist of the hand she had extended towards him and pulled her gently as he moved in on her. He kissed her lovingly, "I want you. I want to put my mouth all over your body." He kissed down her neck, wrapping his arms around her and moving her back to the guest bedroom.

Ophelia pressed her fingers in his shoulders, enjoying his lips on her neck. When they reached the side of the bed he stopped walking. His hands lifted the bottom of her t-shirt and proceeded to take it over her head. He removed his shirt. Ophelia ran her hands over the muscles on his chest and abdomen. Seth was sexy and turned her on to no end. His open mouth kissed across her collarbone and shoulder with his eyes taking a look at the button on her jeans.

His fingers went to the button and zipper but he paused to look in her eyes, "Can I?"

Ophelia nodded, biting her lip. Seth's fingers unbuttoned and unzipped her jeans, his hands pushed the jeans over her hips and they fell to the floor. Ophelia stepped out of them.

He looked down at her and smiled, "I like pink lace."

Ophelia's bra and panties were a soft pink lace, very sexy and touchable. She smiled with eyes beckoning for him to touch her. Her fingers went to the button and zipper of his jeans but she didn't ask. She unfastened and moved his jeans off his hips. Seth was running his hands down the curve of her sides when he kicked his jeans to the side. One hand slipped under the front of her panties and touched her gently. Ophelia held on to Seth's shoulders, pressing her face in his neck. He moved his mouth to hers, tangling his tongue. His fingers moved over her, feeling her warm and ready for him. Ophelia sighed a soft moan, clinging to him and pressing her body against his. Seth's hands took the sides of her panties and pushed them over her hips. He continued to kiss her as he wrapped his arm around her and moved her onto the bed. Seth hovered over her, reaching around her back and unclasping her bra.

He stopped kissing her to look at her breasts while he removed the lace, "You are the most beautiful woman. My God, you are so beautiful."

His mouth kissed down her neck to her breasts where he was gentle at first but with every kiss his lips, tongue and teeth became more determined. He paid close attention to how her body reacted, and the way she reacted excited him more and more. Her soft movements and heavy breaths made him anxious to be inside her.

Seth proclaimed, "I need to be inside you. I can't go slow this time."

Her hands moved to the edge of his boxer briefs and pushed at them until he helped remove them completely.

Her lips pressed against his lips aggressively, "Take me, Seth. I want to feel you inside me."

His body was between her legs ready to thrust, "Are we ok to?" he paused.

Ophelia nodded, "Yes."

Seth moved slowly nudging just the tip inside her. He watched her face, kissing her mouth gently. Ophelia lazily blinked, tilting her head back and exposing her neck.

Seth kissed her jaw line ending at the lobe of her ear, "Nice and easy, baby."

She was tight around him and her body needed time to adjust. Seth didn't push in all the way, instead he pulled out a little and moved back in slowly.

"You fit like a glove." His voice sounded desperate. He continued to work her body with long, slow strokes while he felt her open up to him, enjoying his length. Ophelia's head turned several times while she bit at her bottom lip. She turned, seeking his lips and pushing her tongue to his. Her grasp on him was firm and she moaned into their kiss. Seth picked up the pace, and feeling her body arch away from the bed he placed his hand under her lower back. Ophelia's hands moved to his lower back and then the cheeks of his ass. She pulled him so he would dive deeper and harder.

"Oh God Seth, you are so hard. Don't stop," The deep thrusts of pleasure had Ophelia whimpering barely able to keep her cries hushed.

Seth needed to stop or he was going to be done for. He hadn't had sex in a long time; lack of sex and how much she turned him on was going to do him in quickly. He thrust only twice more and moved out of her. He kissed down her breasts to her stomach and between her legs. His tongue took over where his body left off. His hands cupped the cheeks of her bottom and she was his for the taking. His lips tongue and teeth followed the same routine as he had done to her breasts, first soft and gentle and then forceful, wanting to put her over the top. Ophelia squirmed and panted before crying out. She muffled her sounds with her forearm across her face.

"Baby, don't cover your face. I want to see you."

Seth watched her move her arm away from her face and onto the bed. He slipped two fingers inside her and curved them back towards him. She moaned, turning her face to the side.

His tongue touched the outside of her, "You taste so sweet."

Ophelia's head turned back and forth slowly while the bedding wrinkled in her fingers. He kissed up her stomach to her breasts, letting his fingers pleasure her. He could feel she was getting close but her hand grasped his forearm trying to slow his hand.

"Let me," he whispered kissing her mouth.

Ophelia was short of breath and moved her face to the nape of Seth's neck, hanging on tight to his arm and back. Her entire body felt the tingle as her climax ripped through her. She exhaled hard, breathing into his neck. He felt her body give in and he smiled, kissing her temple. His fingers didn't leave her, they just slowed. Her breathing slowed so he found her mouth and kissed her madly. He moved between her legs again but this time thrust in deep. Ophelia wrapped her legs around him, holding his lower back with one hand holding his shoulder with the other.

His pace was fast and hard and she cried out for him, "Seth, Oh God." She moaned and buried her face in his neck.

When she tightened around him, Seth couldn't hold himself back. His breathing and groaning were felt in her hair. He collapsed on top of her, careful to shift himself a little to her side. He found her lips immediately and kissed her several times.

He lifted to look at her, "Dear Lord, that was something."

She giggled, "Yes it was." She hid her face in his chest.

He rolled to her side, bringing her body with him. Seth held her to him, letting his heartbeat slow and his breathing return to normal. His mind was full of their first lovemaking. Ophelia was a little shy with him, which was a surprise. He noticed she turned her face to the nape of his neck often so he couldn't see her. He loved that she was playful and giggly when he chased after her in the kitchen. Her hands held on to him with need and desire making him feel like she was his. Even with her shyness, Ophelia had struck the perfect balance between letting him take charge and initiating what she wanted. Seth wondered why he had been so nervous to move forward and hated that he had wasted time. This woman was amazing and he was so in love he couldn't help himself; Ophelia would be his.

Ophelia kissed his chest then rested her chin on his chiseled muscles to look at his face, "Are you thirsty or hungry now?"

He looked at her, "Yes, but let me hold you for just another minute."

She put her cheek on his chest, "Your heart has relaxed."

Seth thought to himself that his heart had done no such thing. He knew it never would. They each took a turn in the bathroom. When Ophelia walked in the kitchen she had a long t-shirt on that covered her bottom.

He smiled, "You're a little shy."

"Who eats naked?" She smiled. "You put your boxers on."

"Men are a little different. You on the other hand should walk around naked. Lord have mercy girl, your body is gorgeous."

Ophelia's face turned pink, "Thank you."

He walked over, kissing her blushed cheeks, "I made you blush."

His hands moved under her t-shirt touching whatever he wanted.

"I thought you were eating?" Ophelia lifted an eyebrow.

Seth kissed her lips, "I'm easily distracted knowing you don't have anything on under this t-shirt." He moved back to his food.

"Are you going to eat?"

She shook her head, "No, I ate dinner." Ophelia drank her tea and watched him.

"I don't work tomorrow. If you wear me out tonight, I won't have to run in the morning," she flirted.

He choked on his tea and looked at her. She smiled, waiting for a comment but not receiving one. Seth took another big drink of his tea, wiped his face and washed his hands. He walked to her refrigerator, opened the door and took out a bottle of water that he took a long drink of.

Ophelia watched him, "No comment?"

"I'm getting hydrated." He laughed and scooped her up over his shoulder taking her in the living room. "We are going to break in this couch."

She laughed, "No, it's brand new."

"That's why they call it breaking it in."

He took a blanket and placed it across the cushions, pulled his boxer briefs off and sat down. He took her hand and pulled her to straddle him. She was sitting back on his thighs, each leg on either side of him. He stripped the t-shirt off of her, putting his hands on her hips. He pulled her to him and Ophelia lifted to take him inside her. She was slow gliding him in, kissing his neck and running her fingers in his hair. Her lips met his and she rocked and rotated her hips. Seth's open hands moved over her back and butt, holding her. When her pace sped up he held her hips, pulling down as he lifted his hips to get that much deeper. Ophelia's head fell back and Seth devoured her neck and breasts.

His grip moved to her butt cheeks, "Wrap your legs around me." He stood up, carrying her to press her back against the wall, "Is this where you want to install the book shelf?" He thrust deep inside her.

Ophelia breathy said, "I think so."

He moved in and out of her, "Good choice, nice sturdy wall."

Ophelia giggled, "I'm glad you approve."

He smiled, kissing her several times. Moving them again he placed her on her feet against the back of the couch. His hands touched her face then ran over the front of her body. Seth kissed down her neck and across her shoulder, turning her around. He moved her hair to the side, running his lips down the nape of her neck, then down her spine. He stood back up pulling her against his body; cupping her breasts he kissed the tender spot under her ear. Ophelia turned her face to find his lips. The kiss was passionate, and Seth's hand moved down her stomach, finding the exact spot between her legs that sent her senses skyrocketing. His fingers worked the spot while he watched her chest rise and fall harder and faster. Her hand held his forearm and her body lay back against his.

He moved his lips from hers, kissing her neck, "Is that right? Is that where you want me to touch you?"

Ophelia's head fell back with her neck arching a little, "That's right. Oh my God that's right."

She turned her face to the side, exhaling hard, then turning back to his face and finding his lips. Seth's kiss was long and deep and after his tongue was satisfied, he bent Ophelia over the side of the couch, kissing down her shoulder blade before stepping between her legs to enter her from behind. The first thrust was a slow push until he was as deep as he could go.

He held her at her waist, "Are you ok?"

Ophelia answered with a raspy voice, "Yes."

Seth moved out and back in leisurely and taking his time meant he got to enjoy Ophelia's moans and the feeling of how tight she was around him. She was so sexy, he never wanted to stop making her feel good. When he felt her entire body tighten and let go he slowed and gently removed himself.

"Come with me," Seth said taking Ophelia by the hand. He grabbed the water bottle that was on the kitchen counter and they walked hand in hand back to bed. Seth made love to Ophelia for another hour, moving them all over the bed, completely having his way with her. He loved that she let him do whatever he wanted. She trusted he would be loving and gentle. He was both until he tested the waters to see how hard or rough he could do things to her liking.

When they both were exhausted laying side by side, Ophelia rolled to him, nuzzling against him, "Will you stay the night?"

"Of course. I wasn't going to leave." He kissed her forehead, "You're stuck with me." He wrapped his arms around her.

When Seth woke the next morning, Ophelia had turned away from him, her back pressed against his side. He turned to her, looking at her for a long while. She was beautiful, brilliant, sexy, everything he could ever want. He had a connection and chemistry with her that he had never had with anyone. This was it for him, she was the one, she had always been the one.

He kissed her shoulder and neck, "I have to go home and get a shower. I'm opening the bar." He whispered in her ear.

"No, don't go." Ophelia stretched a little pushing against him. "You don't feel like you want to go." She could feel him hard against her backside.

Seth smiled on her neck and kissed, "You are going to make me late."

He moved between her legs and gently pushed inside her, kissing her shoulder and the back of her neck. He moved in and out of her several times then pulled back, flipping her face up so he could look at her smile before sinking in deep.

"You are beautiful in the morning," He smiled at her.

Knowing exactly what to do from the night before he was going to get her where he wanted her quickly. He adjusted his speed and rotated his hips with perfect precision.

She smiled, "So are you." Ophelia's head pushed in the pillow when her neck arched, "I'm gonna come."

"That's what I want, baby. Come for me."

Seth watched her come undone. In the last tremor of her orgasm he joined her. He gave himself a few minutes to hang on to her before he sat up.

"Ok I'm late, I have to go. You are coming in to see me, right? I'm working behind the bar. I'll save you a seat and feed you."

Ophelia smiled, "Yes, after I visit my mom."

She lay in bed with her head propped up on her hand watching Seth get dressed.

He looked at her smiling, "You watchin' me?"

She bit her bottom lip and dropped her head back on the bed, "You're trouble for me."

Seth walked over to the bed putting his t-shirt over his head, "You're trouble for me." He kissed her mouth several times, "Ok, one more kiss." He kissed her again. "I have to go." He kissed her again. "Stop that." He kissed her again. "You are making me late."

Ophelia giggled, "I haven't touched you. Get your lips off of me and go to work."

CHAPTER 10

Ophelia parked across the street from the Bone and Barrel. The quick stride across traffic brought her to the door that was propped open due to the beautiful weather. Walking in, Ophelia watched Seth talking to a blond woman at the bar. The woman laughed and touched his arm while they spoke. When the blond ran her fingers at the hair by his temple Seth looked up to see Ophelia frozen in the entrance watching. She turned and walked out the door.

Seth got up walking out after her, "Hey, where are you going?"

Ophelia didn't turn around, "Home."

Seth caught her in the middle of the street grabbing her elbow, "Why are you leaving? Come back inside."

"You look busy," Ophelia backed away heading towards her car.

"Come on she's just a girl flirting in the bar," Seth stepped forward coming after her.

"Are they all that familiar? Do they all run their fingers in your hair? You've dated her." She looked at him hoping he would say no.

Seth met her eyes but he couldn't deny it. He had taken the girl out the previous summer.

"Of course you have. This was a mistake," Ophelia said opening her car door.

Seth's voice was stern, "Come back here."

Ophelia got in her car and drove off.

Seth pounded on Ophelia's front door but she wouldn't answer. He walked down the stairs to his car and started honking the horn.

"Jesus, the neighbors are going to freak out." Ophelia said flinging her front door open. She walked to the railing, "What is wrong with you?" She yelled at him.

Seth stopped pushing on the horn and walked up the stairs following Ophelia in the door. She walked to the kitchen, standing at the island and looking through her mail, ignoring him.

"What the hell was that? You don't just walk away from me." Seth looked at her, "That girl doesn't mean anything to me." Seth put his hand over the mail she was shuffling through, "Look at me."

Ophelia turned with a huff and looked at him.

"I'm crazy about you. I don't want anyone else." Seth put his hand on hers.

"And I don't want something everyone else has had." She pulled her hand away. "I don't want other women touching you. I get flirted with all the time and I don't let men touch me. They don't run their fingers through my hair." Ophelia was angry and hated that she was being possessive.

Seth closed his eyes for a moment and nodded, "You're right. I won't let flirty girls touch me. I don't want other men touching you. That won't happen again." His hand moved up her arm until it rested on the side of her neck. His thumb stroked her cheek, "You will never have anything to worry about. I would never step out on you."

Ophelia lowered her eyes and nodded.

Seth continued to stroke her cheek with his thumb, "I know what people say, my so called reputation. People don't know me; they know bartender me. They think because I date, I'm some big player; that I sleep around. I have only been with 4 women and you are one of them.

Only one woman in this town besides you and it was a very long time ago. I am not something that everyone else has had."

Ophelia stepped to him, putting her face on his chest feeling jealous and silly, "I guess I'm a little nervous. I'm sorry."

Seth wrapped one arm around her and his other hand touched her chin, lifting her face so his lips could touch hers. He raked his lips across hers.

"You need to promise me something," Seth looked at her seriously.

Ophelia kept his gaze.

"Your temper goes along with your red hair." He raised an eyebrow, "So we fight, we yell at each other; but you don't run away. We don't walk away from each other. Agreed?"

Ophelia nodded, "Ok."

Seth kissed her, putting her head in a spin. "Come back to the bar with me. I'll feed you and bring you home later."

Ophelia sat at the bar eating and watching Seth work. They talked between customers and every chance Seth had he stood next to her barstool, touching and kissing her.

"I want to take you home and do naughty things to you," he whispered in her ear.

She smiled, "Like what?" She wiggled her eyebrows.

His eyes smiled looking her over, "We need to break in the kitchen. That island has possibilities."

Ophelia laughed.

Later that evening, Seth drove them to her house. No sooner than they walked in her front door he stripped her down and broke in the kitchen. After their exciting lovemaking, Seth spent the night holding her. She fit in his arms perfectly while they slept. When her alarm sounded at 4:30am he woke, kissing her several times.

He joined her in the shower, "How much time do you have?"

"Enough," she said, wrapping her arms around his neck.

Seth whispered, "Mmmm. You feel so good pressed up against me. You gonna let me slide inside?" He picked her up encouraging her to wrap her legs around him. Seth pressed her back to the tile. He kissed her long and slow.

Ophelia could feel him edging to breach her but he continued to kiss her only rubbing her entrance in a teasing way. "Please Seth," she whispered into their kiss.

Seth pushed inside, feeling her clench around him, "You are so tight. Made for me." His mouth ravaged hers while he pounded into her deep and fast. It was no time and Seth was past the point of holding off, "I need you to come baby, I'm close." Seth only managed to plunge inside her once more before he held and groaned, "Fuck." He buried his face in her neck, squeezing her to him, "I couldn't stop, you feel too good."

Ophelia kissed his temple, "I never want you to stop."

Seth sat on the edge of her bed watching her get dressed. Ophelia put her gun in her holster and suit coat over the top, catching an interesting expression on his face.

She smiled at him, "What?"

He shrugged, "You're fascinating."

"How so?"

"You are this gun caring FBI agent and with me you are pink lace and soft kisses, you tell silly stories to my nephews, did I see you reading a law journal the other day?" He walked over, wrapping his arms around her. "You are all kinds of wonderful."

She ran her hands up his chest, "I'm crazy about you."

CHAPTER 11

"Wake up beautiful girl." Seth tickled his fingers down her arm. Ophelia had fallen asleep snuggled against him on the screened in porch at his parent's house. "I need to take you home. We have a big day tomorrow."

Ophelia was hosting friends and family for the fourth of July the following day at her home. They spent the evening at Seth's parents. His dad grilled shrimp and crab for the whole family and his sister, brother in law and nephews were in town for the holiday. They had spent the rest of the evening telling stories and relaxing on the back deck.

"I need a screened in porch, I like sleeping out here. The waves hitting the seawall get me every time." Ophelia yawned, making no attempt to get up.

Seth smiled kissing the top of her head, "You can have anything you want. But right now, I want to get you naked and in bed. Let's go."

Ophelia slowly sat up, "Everyone's gone."

"They went to bed. You fell asleep about an hour ago," he smiled.

Ophelia stood, walking to the screen to look out at the water, "I love the moon on the water. I never get tired of looking at it. So beautiful."

"I never get tired of looking at you." Seth walked to her placing his hand on her upper back. "You are so beautiful, loving. My God, Ophelia I'm the luckiest man."

Ophelia met his eyes, "Seth," she said with a little shyness.

His fingers touched her cheek, "I love you. I've loved you for so long. You make me so happy."

Ophelia placed her hands on Seth's shoulders so he could wrap her up in an embrace. "I love you so much. I feel like I'm home with you."

His lips touched hers, "You are baby; you are."

"How sexy are you?" Shelby walked in Ophelia's front door with a beach bag over her shoulder, strawberry shortcake in one hand and a bowl of fruit salad in the other. Ophelia helped her overloaded arms, taking the bowl of fruit salad.

"Thank you. Is it too sexy?" Ophelia asked. She was wearing a blue and white striped bikini top and red shorts. Owen and Jake charged in, grabbing Ophelia's legs.

"Hi boys! I have bubbles and snap pop fireworks on the back deck for you. Ask Uncle Seth to help you, he's out there with your Grandpa." Ophelia smiled, rubbing their backs. Both boys took off running to the back door.

Ophelia and Shelby made it to the kitchen. Mike walked in, "Where do you want the ice?"

Ophelia smiled, "Thanks Mike, will you take it to the deck. Seth has it in coolers out there. Beer is in the blue cooler."

"Perfect." Mike gave Shelby a quick kiss before walking out to the back deck.

Shelby continued the conversation, "You look great. If I had that body, I would be showing it off too. It's not too sexy; it's a bathing suit. You look beautiful." Shelby assured her.

"I just have friends from the Mobile field office coming, do you think it's appropriate? If it was just us, I wouldn't think twice but?" She shrugged.

"It's a party on a deck with swimming, boating and jet skis. I'm in a tankini. I would wear a bikini but my boys gave me stretch marks." Shelby grimaced.

"Please you're gorgeous and you know it," Ophelia shook her head. "I made us a champagne cocktail with fruit, are you ready?"

"Hell yes! Mike has promised to take care of the boys and then me." Shelby wiggled her eyebrows.

By 2pm most everyone made it to Ophelia's for the party. The back deck, dock and house were full of her friends, co-workers, Seth's friends and a few employees along with his family. Dad Corrigan and Seth manned the grill feeding everyone burgers, shrimp and fish. The women put together delicious side dishes that went along with the main course. Drinks were flowing and everyone seemed to be having a good time. Mom Corrigan found Ophelia in the kitchen getting Owen and Jake cookies.

"They ate their hamburgers so I promised cookies," Ophelia smiled.

"They have you wrapped around their fingers," Mom Corrigan laughed.

"Yes they do. I'm not embarrassed," Ophelia grinned.

Mom Corrigan touched her cheek, "You look happy. It's good to see this house full of laughter and you smiling."

"I remember my parents throwing parties like this. We always had so much fun." Ophelia smiled.

"We did. Your Momma and Daddy knew how to throw a party. All you kids would swim and eat cookies like Jake and Owen are doing. It was and is a great life. I'm proud of you."

Ophelia hugged Mom Corrigan, "Thank you. I hope you're always proud of me."

Mom Corrigan touched her chin, "Oh honey, it's impossible not to be. You're a wonderful woman."

Seth walked in smiling, "Owen sent me in for his cookies. I need cookies too."

Ophelia laughed, "Are you behaving? The boys are being good, ate their burgers. What did you do to deserve cookies?" She teased.

Seth raised an eyebrow scooping her up in his arms, "You better give me some cookies, woman, or you're going in the water."

"Don't you dare. Put me down right now." Ophelia squirmed. "Don't make me put you on your butt."

Mom Corrigan laughed, "Oh do it. Wait let me get Dad." Mom Corrigan walked out on the deck.

Seth lowered Ophelia just enough to leave a wet kiss on her mouth, "You wouldn't really knock me on my butt would you?"

"You wouldn't throw me in the water would you?" She wrapped her arms around his neck.

He placed her on her feet, "Only if you hold out on those cookies." He spanked her butt.

Ophelia added a few more cookies to the plate, "Your nephews get first choice."

Seth smirked, "You love them more than me. I knew those boys were going to be a problem. When they are around, I'm neglected."

Ophelia laughed touching Seth's bare chest, "I'll make it up to you tonight."

Seth grabbed her fingers placing a kiss on them, "Promise? Because you are killing me in that bikini top."

Ophelia nodded.

Ophelia's bay house had a perfect view of the Fairhope Fireworks. All the guests that stayed until dark sat out on Ophelia's back deck watching the explosion in the sky. Seth had stood with Ophelia in front of him near the back door. His arms were wrapped around her middle with his hands tucked under the edge of the t-shirt she put over her bikini when it got dark.

Seth kissed her temple, "I want to make our own fireworks." He whispered in her ear. Taking her by the waist he moved them in the house.

"Seth, everyone is right outside."

"Shhh. We will be very quiet." He walked her quickly into the guest bedroom and then the attached bathroom shutting the door. "Take those shorts and panties off."

"You're so bossy." Ophelia smirked but did as she was told.

Seth picked her up placing her on the bathroom counter top. He stood between her legs giving her a soft kiss, "You like me bossy." His face dropped to her thighs where he kissed. "Open up for me. I need to taste you." Seth's tongue licked her slowly from her entrance to the place he loved to tickle.

"Seth. I'm never quiet when you do that. You can't." Ophelia's head fell back.

Seth smiled, "You taste so much better than those cookies. You don't think you can be quiet?" His lips sucked her in with a little pulsing.

"Ohh. I can't." Ophelia moaned.

Seth pushed his swim shorts down, positioning himself between her legs. Before he thrust inside her his mouth covered hers to muffle the moan he knew would come when he entered her.

His pace was slow and steady so he could enjoy her, "Feel good?"

"God, Yes. Every. Time." She moaned quietly.

"I love you, Ophelia. You're mine. Tell me that you are?"

Ophelia was breathy, "I'm yours, Seth. I love you so much. Oh. God."

Her face tucked into the nook of his neck muffling the soft cries of bliss while her body quaked.

"I love making you come; love making you feel good. You're everything baby, my whole world." His pace quickened and he finished with a heavy groan.

They took a minute holding on to each other.

Ophelia lifted her head listening to the explosions, "That sounds like the grand finale."

He laughed, "Good timing."

CHAPTER 12

"Aunt Ophelia, are you going to tuck us in and read to us?" The boys stood in front of her.

She and Seth were sitting in a chaise lounge on the back deck at Mom and Dad Corrigan's. Ophelia stood, leaving Seth's arms.

"Yes, I am. Did you pick out a book?" She followed the boys in the house, looking back to smile at Seth.

Ophelia sat with her back resting against the headboard of the bed; Owen and Jake snuggled on each side of her.

"Oh this is a good book. Did you know my friend wrote this? I love flying fish stories. And look at this, two boys help her." Ophelia began to read, "Ava the Aviator."

Soon she was interrupted like she always was.

"Aunt Ophelia, did your friend meet this fish?" Jake asked.

"I believe she did." Ophelia smiled.

Aunt Ophelia, "Do you think goggles would stay on a fish?" Owen asked referencing the book.

"I think very sticky goggles would stay on a fish. Maybe the boys should have used some bubble gum along with the shoe strings." Ophelia smiled.

Both boys laughed.

Jake stated, "A stork is just a bird. Birds can't carry a baby."

Ophelia smiled, "Now that depends on the size of bird and the size of baby. A stork is a very large bird."

Owen answered, "The girls at school say a mommy and a daddy have to make a baby."

Ophelia smiled, "Hmmm. Maybe you should ask your Momma about that."

Both boys nodded.

Jake asked, "Are you going to marry Uncle Seth?"

Ophelia raised an eyebrow, "What do you know about getting married?"

Jake smiled, "You get all dressed up and hold hands. The preacher from the church tells you to kiss. Then everyone gets to eat your birthday cake and dance at your party."

"Well that sounds like a mighty fun time." Ophelia almost laughed. "We are never going to get through this book tonight."

Owen laughed, "We never do."

Ophelia tapped his nose with her finger, "That's because you two like to ask me questions."

"Cause you have all the answers. Momma says girls are very smart, she's smarter than Daddy but we shouldn't tell him because it will hurt his feelings." Owen smiled.

"Good call. We don't want any feelings hurt." Ophelia smiled.

"Why aren't you married like Momma and Daddy?" Jake asked.

"A girl has to be asked by a boy. I haven't been asked." Ophelia smiled and turned the page of the book.

"Uncle Seth will ask you. He loves you." Owen smiled.

Ophelia smiled, "Who have the two of you been listening to about all this marrying stuff?"

Owen and Jake laughed, "Momma and Grammy. Uncle Seth told

them, he'd ask when you're ready."

Ophelia laughed, "Hmm you know what I was thinking would be a great time?"

Both of the boys looked at her, "If your Momma had another baby. What about it? You could have a brother or sister, someone else to boss around and do the chores you don't want to do?"

Both boys looked at each other.

"Sounds like a good plan to me. I say you ask your Momma about having another baby or maybe two. Wouldn't it be great if you each had a baby brother or sister of your own? I would definitely ask for two." Ophelia smiled.

Ophelia went back to reading the book unaware Seth stood at the door laughing silently.

The following afternoon Ophelia was on the back deck standing with her arms wrapped around Seth while he manned the grill at his parent's house. He had one arm wrapped around her with his lips finding her forehead often.

"This has been a great weekend with everyone here," he smiled at her.

"It has. I can't believe the summer is almost over. You'll be back in school in a couple weeks." Ophelia smiled.

"My schedule is good Monday, Wednesday, and Thursday; that leaves plenty of time for lazy weekends." He winked at her.

Ophelia smiled at him, "I love you."

His lips brushed hers, "I love you more."

They heard Shelby yelling from inside the house, "Ophelia Griffin, you are in big trouble."

Ophelia turned producing an innocent smile while watching Shelby storm out of the house joining Mom and Dad Corrigan, Seth and her on the deck. Ophelia raised her eyebrow, "You're all worked up. What's the problem?"

"Baby makin'? You suggested that the boys ask me about having another baby? Are you out of your mind? They said two babies, one for each of them." Shelby looked wild.

Mom Corrigan inserted, "I think that's a lovely idea. I want a granddaughter."

Ophelia laughed, "You messed with me first. You know I always win."

Shelby put her hands on her hips, "I have no idea what you're talking about?"

Ophelia walked over to her ice tea and took a sip, "Oh really? Your boys want to plan a wedding. Where would they get an idea like that? The kind where you hold hands, a preacher tells you to kiss and then we can all eat birthday cake and dance."

The entire group started laughing.

"I just suggested that a little brother or sister would be a great idea, taking the focus off of me." Ophelia smiled.

Shelby shook her head, "At least you didn't tell Mike I said I was smarter than he was." Shelby laughed.

"Mike already knows you said that." Ophelia laughed, "Your boys can't keep a secret any better than you can."

"Exactly." The entire group chimed in then broke into laughter.

"Seth, I'm home. Where are you?" Ophelia walked in the door of her bay house after work on Wednesday. It was after 7pm; she had a late evening since the Sipes Family had an outing.

"Upstairs, master bedroom," Seth called down the stairs.

Ophelia locked her guns in the cabinet and changed her clothes to shorts and a t-shirt. She headed upstairs to join him.

"Hi. This looks great." She smiled at what he had accomplished, walking to him offering a kiss. "It's about done."

"Yes it is. We can get you moved in here by the weekend. I'll leave the doors open to air out the fresh paint smell."

"Want a glass of wine?" Ophelia asked.

"Sounds good."

Ophelia went to the kitchen pouring two glasses of red wine from an open bottle. When she returned Seth had the French doors open and was sitting on the floor in front of the doors. He was relaxed, arms back holding him up with his legs extended and crossed at the ankle. She handed him a glass of wine and sat down next to him.

He smiled clinking her glass, "This is a great view. I think you should put the bed right here."

She smirked, "You can't put the bed in the middle of the room."

Seth shrugged, "It's your room, do what you want."

"I think a couch would be good right here. The bed over there." She motioned to the large wall to the right. She took a sip of her wine. "This looks beautiful. Thank you for helping me."

He smiled, "Thank you for letting me."

"The color is perfect." Ophelia looked around the room at a pale blue-gray tone.

"Really good color." Seth smiled, "I have to say, I was worried you would paint your bedroom pink."

Ophelia laughed, "You have a problem with pink walls?"

"Well, I think it would definitely make a statement that it was your bedroom." Seth confessed.

Ophelia nodded, "Not our bedroom?"

Seth's face became serious, "Is this where you want to live? Have a family here?"

Ophelia looked out at the ocean, "I want to raise children on the water. The way we were raised. We turned out pretty good."

Seth nodded, "I want to marry you, give you babies and live in this house. Are you ready?"

Ophelia turned looking in his eyes, "I love you so much. I want to marry you, have your children and live here. But I want to finish the house and enjoy us. I've never been this happy; we don't have to be in a hurry. I'm yours."

Seth took her in his arms, "I love you. You make my life."

Seth made love to her right then and there. His touch and caresses that night were so gentle and sweet they filled her with love that she never knew was possible.

CHAPTER 13

"It's the week before school starts so Mrs. Sipes is taking the girls clothes shopping in Spanish Fort and doing a few errands in Mobile. I don't know what time you should expect me. I'll come to the bar when I'm done." Ophelia spoke to Seth over the phone early Thursday afternoon.

"Sounds good. I love you." Seth smiled at the phone.

"I love you too." Ophelia disconnected the call.

Two hours later Addison Jacobs walked in Bone and Barrel and asked to speak to Seth. The bartender went to the office letting Seth know he had a visitor. Seth walked in the main dining area and saw Addison and the worried look on her face.

"Hey Addison, Are you alright?"

Addison nodded, "Have you watched the news at all?"

Seth shook his head, "No, I've been working in the office. What's going on?"

"Can we sit over here?" Addison walked to an area that did not have customers. "There's a bank robbery in progress in Mobile. Ophelia is in the bank along with the A.G.'s wife and daughters. We have heard from her, she's ok. I just wanted to keep you informed of what is going on."

Seth could feel his heart beating out of his chest. "Where do I need to go? To the bank? Or the FBI office? Where will she be?"

"The customers in the bank are being held by armed men. There is nowhere to go right now. I'm going to stay here with you so I can keep you updated."

"Do they know Ophelia is FBI? She has a gun? Or they have the A.G.'s family?" Seth asked.

"No. There is no indication that the men know who they are. They were just customers doing some banking. Ophelia has removed her earpiece and is blending in. She knows what to do."

Seth didn't know which emotion was running him, anger or fear. He was distraught thinking she could get hurt, or worse, risk her life to protect the Sipes family. He knew it was her job but the reality of it was crashing down around him. He felt angry that her job had the possibility of hurting her.

Addison studied him as he processed the news, "Seth, she is a smart agent. One of the best I've ever worked with. She's not going to take any chances."

Addison's supervisor asked her to talk to Seth. They were monitoring Ophelia's phone and had viewed two unanswered text messages from Seth. They were also concerned that the situation was not contained and the press would leak that the Sipes' family was in the bank.

Seth just sat looking at Addison for a long while. "If the men find out who they have..." He trailed off.

"Let's not jump ahead. Ophelia knows her job and how to make sure everyone comes out healthy."

Mrs. Sipes and the girls walked into the bank with Ophelia escorting them, another agent waited outside. They were standing in the teller line when gunshots were fired and five masked and heavily armed men created complete chaos. Ophelia placed herself between Mrs. Sipes, the girls, and the guns.

112

She looked at Mrs. Sipes, "Give me your purse. We are just customers and you use my name. Stay behind me with the girls between us."

Everyone was instructed to get on the floor; all of the bank customers and employees followed the directions immediately. Ophelia had already located the exits, security and weapons that customers were carrying when she entered the bank. Through the commotion she identified an off duty police officer. Speaking in a low tone, "Blue?"

He nodded.

She pushed her jacket to the side showing her badge.

He nodded.

"Armed?" she again spoke low.

He nodded. "Ankle."

Ophelia nodded, "Shoulder, Ankle."

Neither spoke again but when they were ushered to sit under the bank counter area the officer made sure he was near Ophelia. When they heard the sirens Ophelia closed her eyes for a second, not happy. Everything just changed. Without an exit and the police outside, the five men would make bad decisions in the hopes of not getting caught.

Two hours passed with temperaments beginning to change. The five men were agitated with the situation and each other, anxious for a plan. The FBI had made contact. Ophelia watched all aspects of the situation, she had moved forward slightly, blocking a direct view of Mrs. Sipes and the girls. Two of the men were in charge of watching the bank customers; they were keeping everyone fearful and quiet with the gun wielding and intimidation. The leader hung up the phone and grabbed the female bank manager placing a gun to her head marching her to the front door. With the commotion, the two men that were watching the customers turned to watch their partner threaten the life of the bank manager at the window for the FBI to see.

Ophelia took the opportunity to look back at the girls whispering, "Girls, remember how we practiced. You listen and do everything I say. Quiet as a mouse. Plug your ears and close your eyes and think about riding your horses. Hide your faces in your Momma."

The girls nodded and did as they were told. Mrs. Sipes made eye contact with Ophelia.

Ophelia nodded, "You know what to do."

Mrs. Sipes nodded with fear across her face. She held her daughters close tucking their faces in her body. She positioned herself behind Ophelia.

The off duty officer reached for his ankle but Ophelia spoke up, "Not yet. Wait for the FBI breach. These men would open fire on everyone." She knew the armed men were unorganized and stupid; those two traits would get everyone killed. All of a sudden, one of the security guards rushed forward to tackle one of the armed men that had his back turned. Another armed man turned without hesitation and shot the guard. Screams were heard and customers crouched lower. The security guard stumbled back and fell five feet in front of Ophelia.

She waited for the armed men to stop arguing, making eye contact with one of them she asked, "Can I help him?"

The armed man walked over, pulling the security guard by the arm towards Ophelia. He dropped his arm and motioned with his gun for her to help the guard. Ophelia checked the guard and found a pulse. The guard had been shot in the chest with an exit wound mid back. The off duty officer took off his jogging jacket and tossed it to her. He knew Ophelia could not take off her jacket because she would expose her gun.

Ophelia packed the wound best she could and pressed, "He needs an ambulance."

The armed man shook his head.

"Use him to negotiate. I need to keep him alive for you to do that. I need to pack this wound."

The leader walked away from the door throwing the bank manager to the floor. He gave instructions to another of the armed men, sending him to look for a first aid kit. The phone started ringing and a voice was using the megaphone outside. Chaos again.

Addison hung up the phone and looked at Seth. "Let's wait at Ophelia's." Addison stood, "I'll drive."

"No. I want to go where she will be. Have they been released? Where is she?" Seth didn't stand. He looked up at the television and watched. The gunshot was loud and the TV reporter crouched, taking cover. The news was replaying it over and over.

"Who got shot?" Seth was in a panic and stood, "Take me to the bank."

Addison shook her head, "They don't know. Stay calm. Let's wait for her at her house. It's going to be hours." She took Seth's arm, "It's not her, there would have been more shots fired. She would have used her gun. Stay calm. Call your parents and have them meet us."

The five-armed men stood together arguing and shouting at each other. Ophelia took the opportunity to hide Mrs. Sipes wallet and her FBI badge on the security guard. She wrote in blood on a piece of gauze "5 Armed", stuffing it behind her badge. The FBI would negotiate for the wounded and start working the robbery protocol. This guard would be leaving the bank.

It was almost 8pm when Addison walked in the living room looking at Seth, "A bank security guard was shot. Ophelia is fine along with Mrs. Sipes and the girls. She sent us a message."

"What message?" Seth stood up.

"She hid her badge and Mrs. Sipes' wallet along with a note on the security guard letting us know how many are armed. Ophelia got rid of the possibility of the armed men finding out who they are, they are just bank customers; nobody will know the wiser." Addison offered a considerate nod.

Seth sat back down, running his hands over his face.

Mom Corrigan had tears running down her face, "She's so smart. That was so smart. She's going to be fine. I know it."

It was nearly 2am. Ophelia knew the FBI would breach soon. All protocol had been exhausted and it would be a good time, middle of the night. She could see the signs of what was coming. The five men, exhausted and without a plan, huddled together in the middle of the room frequently. Ophelia started getting prepared, moving back and in front of Mrs. Sipes so that she could take any shots fired or any that would ricochet. She had Mrs. Sipes blanket both sleeping girls with her body and told her to get down low to the ground. Ophelia signaled to the Off-Duty Officer to get ready.

It was 3:30am when Addison walked from the kitchen finding Seth looking out the sliding glass door, "She's out. They are all out of the bank and on their way to the hospital."

"Is she hurt? Anyone hurt?" Seth asked with fear on his face.

"No. It's protocol." Addison smiled, "She's fine. Our supervisor has talked to her. She can't call you. They will debrief her and escort her home when she's done."

"I want to go to the hospital." Seth approached Addison.

"You can't. It's locked down tight. You won't be able to see her until it's done."

At 5:45am Seth heard footsteps on the front porch and the door open. In only a few strides he was at the door.

Ophelia looked at his face and gave him a tender smile, "It's not mine. It's not my blood. This looks very scary, let me change my clothes."

His face had a mixture of concern, fright and a little anger.

He reached for her pulling her to him, "Are you ok? Are you hurt?"

She wrapped her arms around his middle, "I'm ok. I'm not hurt. Let me change my clothes and get cleaned up before I talk to your parents."

He followed her to the bedroom. Seth didn't want her out of his sight. He watched her change her clothes, putting on a t-shirt and pajama pants. She washed her face and scrubbed her hands. Her hair was up in a ponytail.

Looking in the mirror she said, "I look tired." She turned to him, "So do you. I'm so sorry you have been worrying all day." She took two steps and was in his arms. She wrapped her arms around his neck kissing his lips, cheek and neck. Ophelia spoke in his ear, "I love you. I'm ok. You're stuck with me."

Seth held her so tight she could feel his heart still racing.

"Let's go see your parents so they can go home and get some rest." She moved her hands from around his neck to his shoulders.

Ophelia explained the day enough to satisfy Mom and Dad Corrigan so they knew she was fine. Everyone was exhausted and made plans to have dinner together later that day. They all needed some rest.

"Honey, we are just thankful you are ok. We love you." Mom Corrigan hugged and kissed her.

Dad Corrigan hugged her, "Get some sleep. Love you."

Ophelia walked them to the front stairs and watched them get in their car before she turned to go back in the house. Seth was waiting for her at the door.

They walked hand in hand to the bedroom where Seth undressed her and then himself. Ophelia was exhausted but knew he had a need to be inside her, not for the usual reasons of wanting each other but more because he wanted to claim what he thought he could lose. With a mix of emotions – one being distress – Seth made love to her.

When they were finished, he held her tight to his chest, "I can't lose you. I can't."

"You won't. I'm right here." Ophelia kissed his chest, snuggling her body to him. They fell asleep clinging to each other.

CHAPTER 14

It was mid afternoon by the time Ophelia was able to break free from the phone. She had fielded a number of phone calls from work and spoke to Shelby and Mom Corrigan, confirming that she was doing well. Finally dressed and feeling like herself, she went to find Seth. He was standing on the back deck looking out at the water. Seth hadn't gone home, he showered and changed his clothes from the items he kept at Ophelia's. She walked out the sliding glass door, "You're awfully quiet. Think you might want to share what you're thinking? Let's talk about it." She handed him some sweet ice tea.

"I want you to find another career," Seth stated without any hesitation. "I don't want you to risk your life for other people. I don't want you in harms way. You are brilliant, you can do anything but not this. This is dangerous."

Ophelia didn't say anything she sipped her tea and let him get it all out.

Seth went on pacing the deck, "They could have shot you if they knew who you were. Or worse, threatened one of those little girls and then you would have put yourself on the line to protect them." Seth paused and looked at her. She didn't have an expression on her face. "And what about me? What about our life? I can't live without you. What would I do if you were hurt or killed? You can't do this to us, to me. I cannot lose you. I wouldn't survive it. Do you understand? Do you have any idea how much I love you? I can't do it, Ophelia. I can't be the man that gets a call that you aren't coming home. I won't do it. You won't do that to me. I could have been home pacing the floor with our children. You're going to leave me and children to do this job?"

Ophelia was calm, "Woah, woah. Now let's talk about what is, not what could be. First, we don't have children. If we had children different decisions would be made." Ophelia paused, "This was a bank robbery. It had nothing to do with my job protecting the A.G.'s family. It was bad timing. We were bank customers just like the other 20 bank customers. Those men were after the bank's money, it had nothing to do with who I was protecting."

"But who you were protecting didn't make you just one of the bank's customers. This could have gone very wrong." Seth disagreed.

"I know. I'm an excellent agent. I don't take chances. Everything I do is planned and well thought out. We were not in any more danger than the other bank customers." Ophelia paused, "I could have been in that bank with anyone and had the same outcome, walking out unharmed."

Seth looked at her pointedly, "At any time did you think they were going to shoot you?"

Ophelia shook her head, "I was never scared that they were going to shoot me. I was more concerned about a stray bullet if things got out of hand but I was never concerned that they were going to shoot us. They weren't after us, they were after money and we were not standing in the way of that."

"How did you end up with blood all over your clothes?" Seth was not calming down. If anything she was too calm which agitated him even more.

"There was a security guard that tried to take one of the men down and he was shot. That security guard made a mistake because that was not the way to do things. When he needed first aid, I asked if I could help him because I knew he needed medical attention and it was an opportunity to send a message to protect us more by getting rid of our identification." Ophelia paused, walking to him and putting her hands on his sides, holding the loops of his shorts. She looked in his eyes, "Seth, I know what I'm doing. I'm a great agent. I know my job." She offered a soft smile, "The way I am with you, how I want you to take care of me, how I need you; that is not how I am at work. At work I'm not the girl that wants her boyfriend to take the lead. I'm the girl that shouldn't be messed with; I lead. Can you understand that?"

Seth put his hands on her shoulders, "What about when we have a family, you have children, are you going to go protect someone else?"

"When we have children I'm going to protect our children. They need their mother. I would ask for a field office assignment. I would discuss that scenario with you, we would make those decisions together."

"And what about right now? What if you got an opportunity to protect the President or someone that people would be after; would you go?" Seth asked.

"You're asking a hypothetical. I'm not a secret service agent. I don't know what I would do. You and I would need to talk about it, just like I'm talking to you right now." Ophelia looked to see if he was going to say something. He didn't so she continued; "At no point yesterday was I in fear that I would lose my life. You were more afraid for me than I was afraid. I'm sorry that you worried. But you have to know that we could've walked in that bank, you and me. I would've had my FBI badge in my purse. I would've still helped a security guard that was shot. I would still stand in front of a little child if it came down to it. That's just being a good person."

"You're not even upset today, it's like any other day." Seth commented. He watched how calm she was when she spoke to him.

"That's not true. I am upset but for different reasons. I'm upset that you and your parents worried all day. I'm not happy that you're upset with me right now. I'm upset that those two little girls are probably very scared today. I know Mrs. Sipes was very frightened for her daughters, and I doubt she will be doing banking any time soon." Ophelia ran her hands up Seth's chest, getting closer to him, "I want to put your mind at ease. I'm not going to take any chances with my life. I want to share my life with you, my whole life. I don't want that cut short."

Seth nodded, "OK." His voice was gentle.

"All right. Are we good?" Ophelia smiled.

Seth looked at her and kissed her lips, "I'll get there."

She smiled, "Good, because I'm starving and we never have any groceries in this house."

Ophelia returned to work that Monday, taking the weekend to relax. She walked in the small office off of the living room to get the daily schedule and reports from the night agents when her supervisor poked his head in.

"The A.G. wants to see you in his office."

Ophelia knocked on the office door that was open. The Attorney General looked up from his desk.

He stood, "Come in Ophelia." He walked around the desk, "I know I said thank you at the hospital but I needed to tell you again. I am so grateful. My girls are my life. Thank you for keeping them safe."

Ophelia nodded with a smile, "It's my pleasure, Sir. Your girls are very brave. Your wife was a rock and Caroline and Clara did exactly as they were told. How did they do this weekend?"

"A little shaken up but ok." The A.G. smiled.

Ophelia nodded, "To be expected."

"Ophelia, when my time as A.G. is done, I'm going to hire private security. Any thoughts of possibly leaving the bureau?"

"Sir, I think you need a security team. I'm just one person. I've looked and I have some recommendations if I'm not overstepping."

"Not at all. I would like to see whom you think would be a good fit, especially for my wife and daughters. They are going to miss you."

"I would like to stay in Mobile at the field office. I could be available to you for special events. I am going to miss your family. It has been a pleasure to work with you."

"If you need help getting that assignment, please let me know. I will do what I can. Thank you again." The A.G. reached out his hand.

Ophelia shook his hand, "Thank you."

When Ophelia walked out of the A.G.'s office she heard the girls talking in the kitchen and walked to the entrance. Both girls looked up and ran to her hugging her legs.

"Hello pretty girls. How are you today?" Ophelia smiled patting their backs.

Both girls looked up at her.

Caroline spoke first, "I'm good."

Clara said, "Me too."

"That's good to hear. Are you eating breakfast?" Ophelia looked at their cereal bowls.

"Yes ma'am." Both girls skipped back over to the table to finish eating.

Ophelia smiled thinking that they looked good and were not

upset. They were on their normal routine. She turned to walk back to the FBI office but Mrs. Sipes was standing a few feet away.

"Good morning Ma'am." Ophelia smiled.

"Good morning." Mrs. Sipes walked to her and hugged her, "Thank you. I can't tell you how grateful I am to you."

Ophelia hugged her, "It was my pleasure. Are you doing ok?"

Mrs. Sipes stepped back to talk to Ophelia, "I am. I'm jumpy but I'm ok. The girls were back to normal by Saturday evening."

"You were all very brave. It was scary. Give it a little time and you will be back to normal. Did you want to get out of the house today?" Ophelia asked.

"We probably should. Maybe just downtown." Mrs. Sipes smiled.

"Sounds good. Whenever you're ready, just let me know," Ophelia smiled.

CHAPTER 15

Fall semester was in full swing for both Seth teaching at the University and the Sipes children attending elementary school. Ophelia's schedule was full during the weekdays but most nights and weekends were her own. Seth and Ophelia worked on finishing the house during the day on the weekends. The weekend nights were filled with romantic dinner dates. They never missed a First Friday Art Walk touring the downtown galleries with friends. They were happy and head over heels in love for the entire town to see. It was nearly Halloween when Shelby came to town to visit. She and Ophelia decided to get their bicycles out and participate in the annual Fairhope Witches Ride on Main Street. Shelby walked in Bone and Barrel and took a seat at the bar dressed in her witch's costume.

Seth looked at her with a big grin, "Not a truer uniform could be found in all the land." He laughed out loud.

Shelby looked at him with an evil eye; " Shut up or I'll cast a spell on you. Turn you into a toad. Where is your pretty girlfriend?"

"She's on her way. Before she gets here." Seth pulled out a small box and lifted the lid, "What do you think? I think it looks like her. She hasn't given me any hints on the shape of a diamond." The diamond was a large oval with small round diamonds that circled the band.

"What's there not to like? It's gorgeous; she's going to love it.

When are you going to ask her?" Shelby smiled wide.

"I figured I would carry it around and wait for the right moment." He closed the box and put it back in his pocket."

"Get on with it already. We are all waiting." Shelby laughed.

Seth agreed but they were not in a hurry. They were happy and he took Ophelia's suggestion from the summer, enjoying every moment of their relationship. Ophelia walked in dressed witchy with a hint of sexy. She hugged Shelby and leaned over the bar to kiss Seth.

"You look good." Ophelia smiled at Shelby, checking out her costume.

Seth laughed, "I didn't realize Shelby was in a costume."

"Hush!" Shelby wadded her napkin up and threw it at him.

Shelby looked at Ophelia, "You look good too. I love the striped tights."

Seth included himself again, "Me too. I can't wait to take them off you later."

"Seth!" Ophelia looked around to see his bar customers laughing. Her cheeks turned pink.

His eyebrows bounced up and down.

Ophelia and Shelby lined up with their bikes and at least 100 witches to ride the streets of downtown Fairhope. They took the ride down Fairhope Avenue and circled back to stop at the bars that offered witchy drink specials.

"This is so fun," Ophelia laughed. "I'm kind of tipsy. I think I'm going to walk my bike back to Bone and Barrel."

Shelby laughed, "Me too. Mike texted, asking if we wanted the guys to come to us or do we want to go to them. What do you think?"

"Let's go to them. Seth needs to load the bikes in his car anyway." Ophelia smiled.

Seth and Mike sat at the bar watching the witches come and go. Several stopped to talk to Seth, mostly customers and a few girls he dated.

Mike shook his head, "You have far too many girls wanting your attention. How does Ophelia feel about that?"

Seth shook his head, "It's the bar. She knows how I feel about her and that she has nothing to worry about." Seth felt his shoulders being massaged and turned to see a smiling and slightly drunk Kaitlyn.

"Hey Seth! How are you?" Her hands stopped massaging but didn't leave his shoulders. "Are you enjoying all the witches? This is one of my favorite nights in Fairhope."

Seth turned in his barstool so she would remove her hands from his shoulders but turning to face her only made it worse. Kaitlyn placed her hands on the top of his thighs near his knees standing almost between his legs.

"I was hoping to run into you tonight." Kaitlyn looked at Mike, "I have had the biggest crush on Seth. Our schedules just don't seem to work out."

"Kaitlyn, you know I have a girlfriend. It's not our schedules." Seth tried to move her to the barstool next to him, "Take a seat."

"I'm good." Kaitlyn stood hands on Seth's legs, "How serious is it with your girlfriend? Do you date other girls?"

Seth shook his head, "No, I don't date other girls. You probably need a ride home. Are you here with friends?"

"I think my friends are at The Fly Bar around the corner. Do you want to give me a ride home?" Kaitlyn asked.

Ophelia walked up, "Hi Mike, Shelby and I need a ride home."

Ophelia looked at Seth letting her eyes lower to Kaitlyn's hands on his legs. She shook her head and walked out of the bar. Shelby followed her.

"Where did Mike park?" Ophelia asked looking around. "Do you have the keys?"

Shelby shook her head, "No keys. That looked like crap but there's no way anything was going on."

"She was standing between his legs with her hands on his thighs. Really? I mean really? If that was me and some guy was standing between my legs with his hands on my thighs, you think your brother would be happy?" Ophelia waved her hand, "Fuck it. I'm riding my bike home." Ophelia walked back to her bike.

"No, you're not riding your bike home," Seth firmly said walking out of the bar hearing her decision. Mike walked out behind him pulling his keys out of his pocket.

Ophelia looked at him, "You don't tell me how I'm getting home. Go take your friend home."

Seth pulled his key fob out of his pocket and unlocked the car door, "Ophelia, get in the car."

"I'm not getting in your car." Ophelia looked at Mike, "Will you drop me off?"

Mike nodded.

Seth stepped in front of Ophelia, "It was not what it looked like, let's talk about it at home."

"Was she standing between your legs? Were her hands on your thighs? All you had to do was get your ass up and move away." Ophelia stepped around Seth and looked at Mike, "Where did you park?"

Ophelia walked to Mike's car with Shelby following her. Mike looked at Seth, not wanting to make things worse.

Seth raised his head in a nod, "I'll get the bicycles. Thanks for taking her home."

Mike clapped Seth on the shoulder, "It will look better in the morning."

Seth wasn't going to spend the night without her because of something stupid. She was right he should have stood up and moved away but she had to know he would never do what that looked like. He walked up the stairs to Ophelia's front door. He used his key to let himself in. Seth walked into the downstairs bedroom. The moonlight coming in the window allowed him to see her lying in bed on her side turned away from him.

"I know you're awake. I can tell by the way you're breathing, plus you're too angry to fall asleep." Seth said unbuttoning his shirt.

"Go to your home." Ophelia said with conviction.

Seth was calm. He knew he screwed up. She was right; he would have gone ballistic if the situation were reversed.

"You are my home." Seth finished taking his clothes off leaving only his boxer briefs and slid into bed. "I'm sorry. You are absolutely right. I should have moved away. I love you and you have to know I would never cheat. You are the only woman I will ever want. Phe, please." Seth put his arm around her middle, pulling her to him. He kissed the side of her head, "I love you, baby. I'm sorry."

Ophelia turned to him, her face burrowed in the crook of his neck with her hands on his chest. Seth wrapped his arms around her, "I love you; you know that right?" Ophelia nodded against his neck. Seth stroked her hair, moving it away from her face. "You're my baby. I'm yours, Ophelia. Yours."

"Aunt Ophelia, do you like my costume?" Owen asked.

Jake walked over, "What about mine?"

"You boys are the best looking dinosaurs I've ever seen. Are you ready to trick or treat?" Ophelia smiled.

"Yes!"

"Boys, get in the car and we will go." Mike ushered the boys out of the Corrigan bay house.

Seth walked down the stairs with Ophelia and Shelby behind him. They drove to the Fruit and Nut district of downtown Fairhope for trick or treating. The houses on the bay were too far apart for children to walk in their costumes. Seth and Mike hung back walking behind Shelby and Ophelia with the boys running ahead up to porches for candy.

"Looks like things are ok?" Mike asked Seth.

"She's been quiet today. I don't think I'm out of the doghouse. That was so fucking stupid. I should have stood up, moved away." Seth raked his fingers through his hair.

Mike nodded, "Men are not as smart as women."

Seth chuckled, "I bet Ophelia and Shelby would agree."

Ophelia walked up the stairs to her house ahead of Seth. He put his key in the lock and opened her front door, letting her walk in first.

"The boys had fun." Seth wanted her to talk to him. They had barely had a conversation all day.

Ophelia smiled, "Yes they did." She left the foyer for the bedroom.

Seth heard the shower turn on and walked in the bedroom with a bottle of water. He wasn't sure if joining her was a good idea but figured, how much worse could he make things?

Ophelia felt the cool air when Seth opened the shower door to step in. She stood facing the water letting it run over one shoulder and soaping up the other.

"Let me do that," Seth said taking the soap from her.

He lathered his hands and washed and massaged her shoulders

and back. Ophelia sighed, enjoying his touch. When he finished with the soap, Seth poured shampoo in his hands and washed Ophelia's hair, massaging her scalp and lathering her hair to the ends. He turned her around so she would tilt her head back under the water, letting the soap rinse out.

Seth looked at her face, "You are so beautiful." He placed his lips on her forehead for a moment. "Talk to me, Phe. Yell at me, something."

Ophelia's eyes opened giving him a hardened look, "Nobody touches you but me. Don't let it happen again. I won't have it. I know they are flirting and you say it means nothing to you but I don't care; don't let girls in the bar touch you. It looks bad to me and anyone else that sees it."

Seth nodded, "I hear you loud and clear. I'm sorry. Nobody touches me but you. I don't want anyone but you."

Ophelia gave a small nod.

His lips sank to meet hers in a kiss that hopefully showed her how sorry he was.

He kissed to her ear, "I love you more than anything. I would never hurt you on purpose."

"I love you too."

Mom and Dad Corrigan hosted dinner early on the Sunday after Halloween so that everyone could get together before Shelby, Mike and the boys left for home in Birmingham. Dad Corrigan made his famous gumbo that everyone loved. The dinner conversation geared towards holiday plans since the next time Shelby and Mike would be in town was Thanksgiving. The girls talked about Black Friday shopping while the men talked football food.

"Seth have you set the date for the Bone and Barrel Christmas party yet?" Shelby asked.

"No, but I'll check the calendar this week and let you know."

Dad Corrigan spoke up, "Ophelia, how does the Mobile field office look? The A. G. assignment is almost done, right?"

Ophelia nodded, "I'm officially off the A.G.'s detail the Tuesday before Thanksgiving. His new security will take over on Wednesday since the family is traveling for the holiday. I'm still waiting to hear about the Mobile field office. The A.G. is seeing what he can do for a permanent placement.

Shelby looked concerned, "What if you don't get Mobile?"

Ophelia shrugged, "I don't know. I've asked for Birmingham or New Orleans as alternatives. Hopefully it won't come to that. I might be able to stay on at the Mobile Office working a case until an assignment comes up."

"You said the A.G. asked you to go private security." Shelby commented.

"He did but I don't want to protect a family running for Governor." Ophelia answered.

"Nothing has come up for a new assignment?" Mom Corrigan asked.

"Yes, several offers came in over the summer for an early reassignment but they were Boston, New York or DC, and all long-term. I should hear something about Mobile in the next couple weeks. Fingers crossed."

Ophelia didn't want to pour salt in an open wound. She knew Seth was already uptight about her options. They talked several times over the summer when an opportunity would come up; he didn't mince words that the FBI was not his favorite place of employment.

Seth spoke up, "Ophelia has lots of options that don't have anything to do with the FBI."

Shelby looked surprised, "Are you thinking about leaving the FBI?"

"No, I'm not. Seth is voicing his opinion." Ophelia pursed her lips together.

"I can't help it. You're brilliant and can do anything. You have options." Seth looked at Ophelia.

Mom Corrigan spoke up, "Who is ready for pecan pie?"

CHAPTER 16

O phelia drove straight to Seth's house after work on Monday. It was three days before Thanksgiving and what she had to tell him would put a damper on the holiday. She walked in calling out, "Seth."

"Hey Sweetheart, I'm in the living room." Seth was grading papers on the couch with music playing in the background. "How was your day?" He asked, looking up to kiss her.

She kissed him and sat down, "I need to talk to you."

He put the term paper down and looked at her face, "Are you ok?"

"I don't know. Not really." Ophelia hesitated, nervous to say what she had to. She spoke slow, stalling because she knew he was going to be unhappy. "I got some bad news today. The case I've been working at the field office for the past week just closed; I've been reassigned to D.C. until something opens here. I called the A.G. and he tried to pull some strings but there was nothing he could do. It could take up to six months for something permanent to open here. I might be able to come down on a case-by-case basis but nothing to count on. I asked about Pensacola, Birmingham and New Orleans, which are a stretch, the commute would be terrible but I thought at least it would be close; they don't have anything. I have to be in D.C. on December 1st to start work."

"No. Tell them no. Take a leave and wait for the opening." Seth could hear the anger in his voice and tried to calm down. They had several conversations prior to this one discussing her work and that the Mobile field office was what he could live with. She knew he wanted her to make a career change.

"If I take a leave it would be longer. They place active agents over ones on leave. If I don't take the assignment in D.C.; I might not get Mobile. It would hurt my career to take a leave right now. They offered me a supervisor position in D.C. I know if I take the assignment, I'm first in line to come back to the Mobile field office. Can you take a semester off and come to D.C.? You have enough time in that they may give you a leave for one semester."

"Fairhope is our home. All our friends, our family, we just finished the bay house; I don't want to go to D.C. Our life is here. You can do anything; you don't have to work for the FBI. You don't have to work, we have plenty of money."

"It's not about the money. I worked hard to get where I am. I don't want to just quit because of a 6-month assignment. It's six months, one semester, you can come with me so we're not apart."

Seth shook his head, "You're serious." He looked at her with annoyance, "You are a lawyer. You've talked about opening a practice. Why can't you do that? "

Ophelia could feel herself getting upset, "My career is with the FBI right now. I've made no other plans."

"I can't go to D.C. for a semester. Even if I took a leave, what about the bar?" Seth was completely aggravated.

"You have a manager and your dad would help. It's one semester so we are together." Ophelia could hear pleading in her voice.

"Stay here so we are together." Seth countered.

"I'm asking you to come with me. I have to take the assignment or I may lose everything I have worked for." Ophelia was visibly upset.

"I'm asking you to stay so that we can move forward with the plans we talked about. This is our home. We talked about raising a family in the bay house." Seth stood up and started pacing, "Why would you want to leave here and put us on hold?"

"I don't want to leave here. I want the job in Mobile but there isn't one right now. Why can't we compromise? Come with me for 6 months. If the Mobile office doesn't have an opening I'll leave the FBI. That will give me time to work on opening a law practice. I'm not putting us on hold."

Seth shook his head, "I don't want to take a semester off."

Tears welled in her eyes, "Ok. Can you get the same schedule you do now? You would have a long weekend every week. We can have the weekends together."

"Long distance. You want to have a long distance relationship? Weekends? We are in bed together every night, sharing our life. I thought that was what you wanted." Seth was furious.

"I do want that. I don't want to be away from you. I asked you to come with me. You are giving me no choice. It's long distance for 6 months at the most." Her fingers wiped the tears that slid down her face.

"You have a choice and you are choosing to leave me. I'm asking you to stay." His face was furious looking at her.

"I'm not leaving you. I'm trying to keep my career. If you won't go with me, it will only be long distance for six months at the most." Ophelia wiped her face, getting rid of the tears.

Seth was disgusted, "I've done the long distance thing. It doesn't work. If you want to go, let's just call it what it is. You're choosing your career over me."

"I am not. Long distance can work if we want it to. It's for a short time. Why are you being like this? You're not being reasonable."

Ophelia stood up, "Why can't you compromise at all? Why does it have to be all your way?"

"If you love me and want a life with me, you will stay." Seth stood his ground.

"If you love me and want a life with me, you will come with me for six months." Ophelia was angry and hurt, "If I don't have the transfer in six months, I'll quit. I want to have our life here. Please Seth."

"I'm not the one turning our life upside down for a job." Seth was livid.

"What is it with this town? You can't leave it for six months? You can't see me on the weekends for six months? I want you to come with me, but I'll compromise for the weekends. I'll quit if I don't get the transfer, so that we don't lose us. Why can't you just give a little?" Ophelia stood, walking so that she was directly in front of Seth.

"We are going around in a circle and getting no where. I am not going to D.C. I don't want to do long distance; I want you with me every day. Long distance doesn't work. If you go, it won't work." Seth stepped around her and walked in the kitchen, opened the refrigerator and pulled out a beer.

"So what are you saying? If I don't do what you want you are breaking up with me?" Ophelia followed him to the kitchen.

Seth took a drink of his beer. He put it on the counter and looked up at her with anger on his face, "I think we need to take the night apart to think about this."

Ophelia couldn't believe her ears. How could he say that to her? As furious as she was with him weeks ago, he wouldn't allow them to sleep apart. "You are punishing me, casting me out because I won't do what you say when you say it?" Ophelia waited for him to reply. Nothing. She walked back to the couch picking up her purse. She didn't say anything or look back when she walked out of his house.

Ophelia didn't hear from Seth on Tuesday. On Wednesday afternoon she waited at his house for him to come home from school. When he pulled up she could tell by the look on his face that he hadn't changed his mind. He looked angry and disgusted with her. When he got out of the car he didn't make an attempt to touch her.

"I guess you didn't need just one night apart?" Ophelia looked at him.

"I didn't know what to say to you yesterday. I don't know what to say to you today." Seth looked down.

"You say that we will work it out no matter what. That's what you say to me." Tears spilled out of Ophelia's eyes. "Did you ask the University if they would give you a semester off?"

"I don't want to take the semester off. I didn't ask." Seth said softly, "Please, don't go."

"Will you work with me on a schedule for weekends and your breaks? I'll come here and you come there." Ophelia wiped her tears.

Seth looked at her, "Let's see how things go."

"What does that mean? You want to break up? You don't want me anymore?" The tears were coming quickly and falling down Ophelia's cheeks.

"Of course I want you. I love you. But I don't think we can make this work long distance. Why should we have to be apart when you have a choice? I'll resent it." Seth closed his eyes, hating what he said. He thought that if he stood his ground she would do what he needed her to.

Ophelia couldn't say anything. She knew if she did, she would completely fall apart and she wasn't going to do that in front of him. She got in her car and drove home to pack.

"Mom Corrigan, are you home?" Ophelia walked in the Corrigan Bay house.

"In the kitchen sweetheart."

Ophelia walked in finding Mom Corrigan elbow deep in piecrust. "I'm getting the pies ready for the oven. How does pumpkin, pecan and apple sound?" She looked up, smiling at Ophelia. Her smile faded looking at the blotching pink tone around Ophelia's eyes. "What is it sweet girl?" Mom Corrigan wiped her hands on a towel, walking to Ophelia and taking her in her arms.

Ophelia hugged Mom Corrigan with all that she had, trying to calm the sea of emotion so she could talk, "He broke up with me. I have to take this job and he broke up with me. If I don't report on the 1st, I will lose my status and rank. Seth won't work it out with me." Her voice was laced with sobs.

"Ok, ok. Let's talk this out. Figure it out." Mom Corrigan rarely witnessed Ophelia in a complete meltdown. Even when dealing with her mother and father, she shed countless tears but rarely resorted to hysterical crying. Mom Corrigan rubbed her hand over Ophelia's back to soothe her. "Come on, I'll make some tea and we'll talk."

"Ok." Ophelia wiped her tears, stepping back. After the situation was explained, Ophelia looked at Mom Corrigan, "I'm going to leave in the morning. I can't be here for Thanksgiving. Look at me, I'm a mess."

"We are your family, Ophelia. You have every right to be here for Thanksgiving. Maybe Seth will get a good nights sleep and think different in the morning."

Ophelia shook her head, "You know your son. Do you really think he will? I was hoping he would compromise but it's been three days and he won't budge. He's pushed me out. Until Monday we hadn't spent a night apart since June. He's punishing me." She shook her head, "I'm leaving tomorrow. I love you and Dad. I want you to have a nice Thanksgiving and I'm not the best company." Ophelia wiped her tears away again before standing. She took her teacup to the kitchen sink saying, "I'll call Shelby tomorrow."

Mom Corrigan nodded. "Call me as soon as you land so I know you're safe."

"I will." Ophelia hugged Mom Corrigan tight.

Ophelia called Shelby from the airport on Thursday morning.

"I thought you would be here by now." Shelby said, looking at her watch she saw it was 11am. "I thought we could catch up and drink mimosas."

Ophelia turned off her feelings so her voice sounded steady; "I'm not going to make it today. Please give the boys a big hug and kiss for me and say "Hey" to Mike for me. You and I will have to catch up another time."

"What? Why can't you make it? Are you sick? Do you want me to come over?" Shelby held the phone, shocked.

"No, I'm not sick. I'm at the airport. My flight was just called. I'll explain everything soon. I love you, Shelby. I'm sorry." Ophelia hung up.

Shelby walked into the kitchen where her mother was cooking, "Did you know Ophelia wasn't coming?"

Mom nodded, "She came to see me yesterday."

"Seth?" Shelby was ready to lose her mind, "Is Seth coming to dinner?"

"I'm not sure. I haven't heard from him yet." Mom continued to cook up a storm.

"Are you going to tell me what happened? Ophelia is catching a flight to where?"

Mom nodded, "D.C., she has to report to work on December 1st and she decided to leave now to get settled."

Mom continued telling Shelby what Ophelia had told her. Shelby poured her second drink, "I'm going to tell Mike I'm going to D.C. for the weekend."

Mom nodded, "I can help with the boys. I think that's a good idea. She is heartbroken."

"I could kill Seth." Shelby looked at her phone to get the time. "She should be landing in about an hour. I'll get my flight and leave her a message."

"Your brother has broken his own heart. Don't be too rough on him." Mom looked at her with pleading eyes, "They are both very hurt. There is no way Seth is handling this well."

It was nearly 3pm when Mom called Seth, "Dinner is at 4 o'clock sharp. Get over here."

"I don't feel up to it." Seth responded.

"Get over here or I will pack up this dinner and bring it to your house." Mom demanded.

Seth walked in his parent's house looking exhausted and red eyed.

"In the kitchen, Seth," Mom called hearing the front door open and close.

Seth stepped to the edge of the kitchen watching his mother preparing the serving dishes.

"I need your help with the turkey." Mom pointed, "The electric knife is in that drawer."

Seth started to carve. "Did you hear from her?"

Mom nodded, "I spoke to her yesterday. She called Shelby today from the airport."

Seth looked at his mother, "She left?"

"Sweetheart, you broke up with her. What was she going to do, stick around a few more days hoping you change your mind? She starts a new position next week and needed to get settled in her apartment. Ophelia couldn't see a point in coming today and making everyone as miserable as the two of you."

Seth put the knife down and walked out of the kitchen to the back deck.

Mom joined him outside. She handed him a beer. "Supper can wait a few minutes. Are you sure about what you're doing?"

Seth looked at his mom, "I'm not wrong. Our life is here. I asked her to stay here. She doesn't need that job; it's dangerous anyway."

His mom looked at him thoughtful, "Do you know how hard she worked to get where she is? She is an FBI agent at 30 years old, a great one. She was given a promotion and assigned to a city that most agents want to work in. Do you know what she wanted? To be in Mobile, Alabama so she could be with you. Nothing goes on in Mobile, Alabama, not like in D.C. Mobile is a step down from where she is. She would take the step down to be with you but she needed time to transfer here. All she asked you for was 6 months so she didn't have to walk away from her entire career, everything she worked for."

Seth looked at his mom, "I want to marry her. I want her to have my children, raise them here. I don't want her working for the FBI."

"So you try to force her hand by breaking up with her? And if it backfires? What then? Are you willing to lose her completely?" Mom touched his shoulder gently, "Seth, be very careful with what you're doing. Go see her. If you don't want to take a leave from work, work out seeing her on the weekends. Don't end things and hurt her like this, you may not get her back."

Seth ran his hand over his face, "I can't do long distance."

"That is baggage you are carrying around. Ophelia is not Carolyn. You are making Ophelia prove her love by giving up what she has worked for. That's not fair."

Seth closed his eyes, "I don't know."

"I love you but you're wrong about this." Mom kissed his cheek and left him on the back deck.

Ophelia reported to work on December 1st. She was busy with introductions and reviewing open cases. The first week went by quickly with her spending 12 hours at the office each day. The time she was putting in wasn't expected but she offered it up without hesitation since she had no reason to go to her apartment. She was lonely and missed Seth terribly. Every night ended the same way, tears and finally a restless sleep. He had sent her several text messages, none of which gave her any hope that he would come to D.C. The messages were more to make sure she was safe and he ended each message with "I love you." She figured the messages were genuine but had a purpose of keeping her missing him in the hopes she would come home. Ophelia picked up the phone to talk to Shelby almost every night.

"Hey Phe, just wanted to say good night. How did you do today?" Shelby hoped to hear a change in her best friend's voice.

"Everything is fine at work. How are the boys?" Ophelia asked.

"They are good. You sound tired. Have you talked to Seth?"

"I am tired. No just a couple text messages. I'm miserable here. I can barely fall asleep and when I do, my alarm goes off to get up. I want this job but I want your brother more. I'm so upset with him. What do I do? Give in? I'm scared to do that; what if I resent him for forcing me to make the decision to leave the FBI to keep him?"

Shelby didn't know what to say. "Think it through. I don't know what to say. You have to decide what you really want. I'm scared that you'll be miserable if you stay and if you go home right now and give up your job, will you be angry with him back home?"

Ophelia's voice was soft and Shelby knew she was crying when she spoke, "I don't want to live here or anywhere without him. I don't want to be stubborn and ruin us but I don't want to let him walk all over me. How will he respect me if I do that? Have you talked to him? Is he upset? Does he even miss me?"

"Ophelia, my brother is in love with you. He's moping. Momma said he's difficult to deal with and his staff is wishing he would take a vacation. I wish I had the right answers. Give yourself a little time to figure out what you want to do. Maybe Seth will come there." Shelby offered.

"I don't think he will." Ophelia knew that.

She could tell by the way he spoke to her that he wasn't going to come to D.C. They ended the call and Ophelia lay in bed wanting Seth to be with her. She read the last text messages he sent and decided to send him a text message.

Ophelia: I love you Seth. I can barely breathe without you. Please come to D.C. when school lets out.

Seth: Come home. Come home to me. I love you. Our life is here. I'm waiting for you.

On December 20th, Ophelia walked to the door of the bar, smoothing her dress before she pulled it open. Bone and Barrel was packed full of customers enjoying the Christmas decorations when she stepped inside. She walked to the corner of the bar rail looking around for Seth. She was meeting Shelby but knew that it would be a few minutes before Shelby arrived. When she spotted him at a customer's table, Ophelia watched some girl dangle mistletoe over Seth. Seth let her kiss his cheek and the girl hugged him putting her lips to his neck.

Seth took her arms in his hands and moved her back slightly. He smiled saying "Merry Christmas."

A moment later he turned to walk away from the table, shocked to see Ophelia watching him from the corner of the bar. Seth could see by the look on her face she had witnessed the mistletoe. Walking quickly towards her he maneuvered through the crowd, making it in time to follow her as she walked out of the bar to the sidewalk on Fairhope Avenue. The cool air and concern of what Ophelia would say rushed to Seth's face, sobering him.

"Ophelia, that was not an appropriate thing for me to do. I'm sorry."

Tears spilled out of Ophelia's eyes she was already anxious about coming home and to walk in seeing what he allowed made her feel even worse. "How could you do that? All of our friends watching you, how could you embarrass me like that."

He reached for her taking her arm so she would look at him, "Ophelia, I screwed up. Everyone knows how miserable I've been without you. It was a kiss on the cheek. Harmless. I had no idea she would hug me. I moved her back."

Ophelia was hurt and angry and without catching her emotions she slapped Seth across face, "Stay away from me."

Ophelia walked down the street to her car, got in and drove away. Seth stood outside in a daze from what just happened. He could feel the heat on his cheek.

Several minutes later, Shelby walked up finding Seth in front of the bar, "What's wrong? Where's Ophelia?" Seth had his hands on his knees looking down. He had remained outside feeling sick.

Seth told her what happened. "I've been drinking. I've been so angry with her for leaving. I don't know why I let that girl kiss me; to get back at Ophelia for taking the job? Fuck I don't know what I'm doing."

Shelby shook her head, "She left the FBI. Came back here for you. Ophelia gave up everything she worked for to be with your sorry ass. She wanted to surprise you that she was home before Christmas. Christ, Seth how could you do that?" Shelby stood looking at him, "I'm going to her house."

Seth looked at her, "I'll go. I'll explain myself."

"She gave you what you wanted, what you forced her to do. Ophelia should have never done that." Shelby pointed her finger at her brother, "I love you, you're my big brother and I will always love you but when is this bullshit going to end? You have been the biggest flirt, needing attention from girls in this bar like it's some sort of game? Ophelia told you no more with the girls after the last time she walked in on someone with their hands on you. When are you going to grow up?"

Seth looked at his sister with shameful eyes.

"You need some coffee. The last thing you should do is talk to her while you are half drunk. Don't you dare go over there tonight. Call Mike to pick you up, you don't need to be driving. You'll be lucky if you didn't lose the best thing that has ever happened to you." Shelby walked away.

Seth pounded on the door of the bay house at 8:00am the next morning, waking Ophelia who had not fallen asleep until very late. Shelby had come over after the mistletoe debacle and they sat up talking and crying until well after 2 am. The pounding shook the house or at least that's what it felt like to her. She put a sweatshirt on over her tank top and left her pajama pants on. Her hair was quickly pulled back in a ponytail and she headed for the kitchen to get a cup of coffee. She stood at the kitchen island listening to the pounding at the door in the hopes Seth would exhaust himself and go away. After another 20 minutes she opened the door. She didn't step aside but he inched his way to the inside standing only in the foyer. Ophelia made no attempt to move them any farther from the door. Seth would not be staying. He stood facing her; she had backed up enough that she was not within his reach without him stepping toward her.

"Ophelia I made a mistake, I am very sorry. Can we sit down and talk?" Seth looked like he barely slept.

"You can say whatever you have to say right here," Ophelia stated with a sober face showing no sign of emotion.

He knew she had been crying, her eyes told the story, but at this moment she was strong standing in front of him.

"I don't know why I let that happen last night. I've been upset with you for leaving and I was drinking. I've been drinking too much lately. You know that girl meant nothing, it was stupid and hurtful to you and I'm so sorry. I know we can work things out, you're home; we can get back on track. I swear nothing like that will every happen again." Seth stood waiting for her to say something.

She looked at him and her eyes had lost the smile that they usually held for him. The pale green of her stare was vacant, "Are you done?" She paused, raising her eyebrows and giving him a chance to say something else before she continued, "If you have said everything you need to, please leave." She pulled the door, opening it further for him to walk out.

Seth looked at her shocked, "No, I'm not done. I want us to talk and figure this out together."

"Together?" Ophelia looked at him with an unfeeling smirk. "You don't want to figure things out together. I tried to do that a month ago; we are not together. You broke up with me and I was a fool to hang on. It's over."

"No, I never wanted that. I just wanted you to be with me, stay with me. I love you. I want our life." Seth tried to touch her but she pulled her arm away from him.

"You want a life on your terms only. We are not partners. In order for us to be together, I had to sacrifice everything I worked for to prove my love to you. You had my love all along but that wasn't good enough. You can't love me the way I deserve. I want a partner, someone that will do what is best for both of us not just for him. You are not the man I thought you were." Finally tears fell from the corners of her eyes. "You need to leave. It's over." Her words cut him down.

"Ophelia don't do this. I know I've messed up. The girl, the way I handled everything; I can make it right." Seth pleaded.

"The girl. There will always be some girl that tries to test you, see how committed you are. It happens to me too, some guy testing the waters to see if I'll cheat or leave you for him. I've never given anyone the time of day but there is something in you that can't seem to stay true to me. Respect me. So this isn't about the girl, this is about you, who you are. You are selfish and I want you gone." She was crying hard now and hysterically said, "I gave you everything. All of me. I let you destroy the love I had for my career, take my joy. I hated the job in D.C. because you made me feel alone. You made it wrong for me to want to hang on to something I worked hard to achieve." She wiped her tears and the hiccup in her sobs made the next words sound that much worse, "Get out of my house. Leave me alone. You have ruined my heart." She placed her hand on his chest pushing him towards the door. "Don't come back. You are free to do whatever you want with whoever you want."

When Seth stepped backwards through the doorway onto the porch, she slammed the door and he heard the click of the lock.

He slapped the door, "No, Ophelia. I want you, only you baby. Please open this door. I was wrong. Wrong about everything. I can't lose you."

His words went unanswered.

CHAPTER 17

Seth walked in his parents house early Christmas morning looking tired and lost. His nephews ran to him hugging his legs, excited to open Santa's presents.

In an excited shrill, Owen said, "We have been waiting for you Uncle Seth. Santa came and brought all kinds of things. Can we open our presents now?"

Seth smiled at both of them patting their backs, "Good morning men, Merry Christmas. Ask your Momma and Daddy if it's time. I'm going to get a cup of coffee and meet you by the tree."

Both boys with excited voices said, "Merry Christmas." They ran to find their parents yelling, "Uncle Seth is here."

Seth made his way to the kitchen and poured a cup of coffee.

His dad stood next to him, "I'll take a refill."

Seth poured coffee in his dad's cup.

"You get any sleep?" Dad asked.

"A little. I'm fine." Seth took a sip of his coffee.

Dad's hand patted his shoulder. He knew his son was as far from fine as anyone could be. His tired, sad eyes looked as if he had cried for days.

"I love you, son."

"I love you too. Merry Christmas, Dad."

"Merry Christmas."

Seth and his Father walked in the living room and watched two eager little boys stacking up presents to hand out. Seth shook his brother-in-laws hand, kissed his sister and mom and sat down near the tree to watch the boys destroy the wrapping on the gifts. After shrills and shrieks of joy and silly giggles the boys had managed to open everything in record time. The adults had opened a few gifts that the boys had made but agreed years ago that they would not exchange gifts since everyone bought whatever they wanted and needed for themselves. The gift giving was for the children and the time together loving one another was for the adults.

"We bought this present for Aunt Ophelia." Owen held it up handing it to Seth. "I asked Momma to take us to the store, she really needs it."

"I'll make sure she gets it." Seth took the wrapped gift.

Jake added, "It's glue. Momma said her heart is broken. We want her to fix it. She's sad and her story telling is not good. She didn't laugh when we read together."

Seth could feel himself getting upset, "You both are kind boys. Give Aunt Ophelia a break on the story telling, ok?"

Owen came over sitting on Seth's lap, "She had to go see her friend that is getting a baby from a stork. Aunt Ophelia said she would take a picture of the stork for us."

"If she said she will get a picture, you can count on it."

Seth was having a hard time holding back tears. Between losing her and lack of sleep, his feelings were raw. He felt like a piece of him had died. Ophelia refused his phone calls and did not respond to any of his text messages. Seth gave her Christmas present to Shelby, asking her to give it to Ophelia, but Ophelia refused to take it. She left the gift with Shelby to return to him when she came to see the boys before she left for New York.

"Are you sad Aunt Ophelia had to visit her friend?" Jake asked.

"I am but Aunt Ophelia will enjoy seeing the new baby. We shouldn't be sad on Christmas. Why don't you pull your train track out and I'll help you put it together." Owen hopped off of Seth's lap and joined Jake on the floor.

Jake nodded, "If your heart is broken, Aunt Ophelia will share her glue."

Seth got up and walked in the kitchen for more coffee. His eyes had glassed over with tears spilling on his cheeks. He had been doing his best not to let them escape but it was no use. He wiped them away while he poured more coffee and started a fresh pot.

Mom walked in the kitchen, wrapping her arms around him, "I'm sorry you're hurtin'. Give it some time; let things ease up a little so she can hear what you say to her. Give yourself time to think things through to say the right thing. She's lost right now, doesn't know what to do. Give her time to figure out what she really wants."

"She didn't go back to the FBI? Is she coming back here?" Seth asked.

Mom shrugged, "I don't know what she will decide. She can go back to the FBI if she wants. She spoke to her supervisor and they not only offered her the job she had, but her choice of another city if she would come back. Mobile still isn't available, not that she would have taken it. She decided not to make any decisions right now. All she wanted was to go to New York for Christmas to visit with her friend and the new baby."

"She gave Shelby my house key to give to me and asked that I give hers back. Ophelia didn't open my Christmas present. I bought her diamond earrings to match her engagement ring." Seth stopped talking for a moment knowing he was on the verge of breaking down.

"I've carried her ring around for two months, waiting for the right time to ask her. At this point she has no intention of working anything out with me. She has completely cut me off." Seth's tears streamed down his face. "There will never be anyone else for me."

"She still loves you or she wouldn't be this upset. Give her some time." Mom patted him.

CHAPTER 18

Ophelia returned to Fairhope on January 2nd for a meeting with a real estate broker she contacted while in New York. They met at an available upper storefront on the corner of Fairhope Avenue and Section Street with parking in front and on the side. They took the stairs to the outside entrance and entered the space. The walk through went quickly since the space was an open floor plan with two bathrooms near the rear exit.

Ophelia smiled at the broker, "Ask the landlord to send over the lease agreement and I'll review it."

"You'll take it then?"

"Yes, as long as the numbers in the lease come back as we talked about. Any idea what the owner is selling the building for?" Ophelia noticed the "Building for Sale" sign when she parked. "Can you get the specifics on the purchase price, outstanding debt and how long the businesses in the building are leasing for?"

"I'll get the details over to you as soon as possible. I hope to have the lease to you this afternoon."

"Perfect," Ophelia shook the brokers hand.

When she walked outside she took a look at the storefront and building with a smile.

Next up for the day was a new car. She drove to the dealership and traded in both her parent's cars and her car from her college days and pulled out of the dealership with a brand new silver, Mercedes CLK 430 convertible. It was too cold in January to put the top down but she would love it come spring. While in New York she had researched available office spaces, filed the proper paper work to start her law firm, and looked for graphic designers for a website and marketing materials. She even figured out what she wanted to drive and had the dealership get the car ready. Ophelia was determined to accomplish everything she had put off for years. She figured that if she stayed on task and busy, she could keep Seth and her feelings at a distance. There would be no more public displays of feelings. She knew how to be stoic, push feelings down so that she didn't embarrass herself or give anyone the impression she didn't have it all together. The exception was when she visited her mother; she could never hide how she felt. She wished she could talk to her about everything that had happened to hurt her over the last several weeks. She wished for advice, her mother was always good at giving her just enough that Ophelia would make good decisions on her own.

When she arrived at Homestead Village, her mother was in her room, sitting in a chair, looking out the window. The nursing staff had told Ophelia that her mother was having a difficult day.

Ophelia knocked on the door, "Mrs. Griffin, may I come in?"

Ophelia was holding a bouquet of mixed flowers in a vase. Her mother looked at her, unsure if Ophelia was talking to her. She was completely lost as to who and where she was.

Ophelia walked in, "That's a pretty pink sweater."

"Thank you." Ellie looked at what she was wearing then back out the window.

Ophelia put the vase on her dresser and moved a chair near her mother. They sat in silence for more than an hour.

"Are you hungry?" Ophelia asked.

"Yes, I am."

"It's time for tea and cookies. Come with me."

Ophelia led the way to the patient cafeteria and Ellie walked in, taking a seat at a table with other patients. She hadn't noticed Ophelia didn't sit down. No matter the heartbreak she felt over Seth, watching her mother like this was pure torture. The pain was something she couldn't describe. It was a loss that she was still losing, slow and painful torture. Ophelia knew what the doctors said but every time she visited she hoped her mother would know her if only for just a moment, but she hadn't in 3 1/2 years. Ophelia found it difficult not to keep track of the time since her mother last recognized her. She left their visit broken hearted but felt relieved that it wasn't because of Seth.

When Ophelia returned home the driveway looked very large with only her car parked on the concrete now. The lease for the office space was in her email along with the details for the purchase of the building.

Ophelia stalled the lease for a couple days in order to get contractors lined up for the renovations and to look at the overall building for maintenance and repairs if she decided to purchase it. The lease came with 60 days of free rent allowing for renovations, and she wanted the doors to open before that free rent period ended. It would be a mute point if she decided to buy the building but wanted to keep her options open until she had all of the information regarding the purchase. The next few days were filled with graphic designers, sign companies and decisions on the renovations and purchase.

"Hi Dad Corrigan, can I get your help with something?"

"Of course, what do you need?" Dad was happy to hear from Ophelia.

Ophelia gave him the details of the building, which he was

already familiar with. There weren't that many buildings for sale downtown. She met him to walk through the office space and look over the information the contractors gave her.

"Can I buy you a cup of coffee at R Bistro? We could look at the estimates for repairs and see what you think. I'm not sure about the purchase of the commercial space and need some good advice."

Dad Corrigan smiled, "I would love a cup of coffee." He put his arm around her shoulders and kissed the top of her head. "Is this what you really want?"

"Yes. I don't want to leave my mom. I want to be close to you and Mom Corrigan. I want to enjoy Shelby's boys. Fairhope will always be my home."

Dad Corrigan smiled. "And Seth?"

"I can't talk about him." Ophelia stated without emotion.

Dad Corrigan nodded, "I'm glad you're home. Mom will be thrilled."

Seth had called or texted every day since Christmas without receiving a reply. His latest text message lit up her screen while at RBistro with Dad Corrigan.

Seth: I know you're home. My mother said your Mom has fresh flowers and you are with my Dad. Please let me see you. I love you.

Ophelia read the message and again chose not to reply. She put her phone back in her purse.

Dad Corrigan looked at her, "Do you need to get that?"

"No. It's fine."

Ophelia listened to Dad Corrigan tell her the building repairs were minimal and he knew a couple contractors that would bid the jobs for a lower price. Ophelia smiled, getting the information that she needed. She would buy the building; it was better than paying rent.

"Was it Seth on the phone?" Dad Corrigan asked.

Ophelia nodded, "Every time I think of returning one of his messages, all I have to say is something ugly and hurtful. My mother would tell me that if I didn't have anything nice to say I shouldn't say anything. It was good advice, so I'm taking it."

Dad Corrigan patted her hand, "You're going to do amazing things with this building. Take a little time for yourself to concentrate on you and being an attorney, maybe you will think of something nice to say to Seth."

CHAPTER 19

"Are you staying at Ophelia's?" Seth asked his sister. "No, I'm staying with Momma and Daddy. They are going to help me with the boys; Michael had to work and couldn't come. I didn't want to worry about the boys while I'm helping Ophelia with the move into her office."

Shelby came in town the Thursday before Ophelia was set to open the doors of her new law practice that Monday.

"I can help with the boys." Seth offered.

"That would be great. Are you ok?" Shelby asked.

"I'm hoping maybe you can convince her to talk to me." Seth was desperate.

"You know her, there is no convincing Ophelia. Give her time. She can't keep her feelings shut down forever."

Shelby didn't know what to tell Seth. She felt between a rock and a hard place. Ophelia refused to show any emotion let alone talk in detail about Seth and how she felt.

"It's been a month and a half." Seth was angry, mostly with himself. "It's fucking February. Not one word. I could beat her door down and she wouldn't answer. I've sent every gift, every flower, food, dropped off groceries. Hell I'm throwing a fundraiser for James Sipes for his run for Governor. What do I do?"

"Maybe stop. Let her be. Give her some time without you doing all of this. Obviously it's not working." Shelby was clueless for an idea.

"No. I'm scared she will..." Seth stopped.

"She's not going to forget about you. Ophelia is not over you Seth. She is sad. I can hear it in her voice. I'm just saying that maybe stop throwing salt in the wound, let things heal." Shelby offered.

"Just talk to her. See if you can convince her to have a cup of coffee with me." Seth was aggravated.

Shelby's visit was productive. She helped Ophelia pick out paintings from local artists that they decorated the law office with.

"This is very beautiful. Sophisticated." Shelby smiled, looking around the office.

"Thank you. I love the way it has turned out. Now I just need some clients." Ophelia gave a half-hearted smile.

"I don't think that is going to be a problem. Starting with the Sipes' family is pretty good." Shelby walked through the office with Ophelia evaluating every room.

"I'm just looking over some contracts and financial documents for his campaign." Ophelia replied.

"My brother is hosting a fundraising event for Mr. Sipes at the bar." Shelby watched Ophelia.

Ophelia nodded, "I heard. I had lunch with Mrs. Sipes and the girls last week."

"Won't you talk to him? It's obvious you are sad, I have barely seen you smile. What about just hearing him out? Do you miss him?" Shelby asked.

Ophelia missed him more than she thought she could. Not having him involved with her life and the changes she made was difficult, from the moment they got together she thought they would never be apart.

Ophelia's eyes glassed over, "I can't. Your brother hurt me so much. I just can't."

"Maybe you need him to take that hurt away?" Shelby hugged her. "He loves you so much. What are you going to do? Stay like this?"

Ophelia shrugged, "I don't know."

"Can you get over him? Move on?" Shelby asked pulling back to look at Ophelia's face.

"I don't know how. I'm stuck." Tears rimmed her eyes but she would not allow them to flow, "I can't go back and I can't move on."

Shelby broke the hug, "You need Owen and Jake to give you some hugs and kisses. Let's go."

Ophelia spent the evening with the little boys who snuggled with her, overwhelming her with love that she desperately needed. She read them a book, the boy's style, which meant more questions than book reading.

Seth stopped by his parent's house before Shelby left to give his nephews and sister a proper send off on late Sunday afternoon. The boys were all over him until Grandpa pulled up a crab trap. Jake and Owen went running out the door to the dock.

Shelby looked at Seth who was watching her boys; "I talked to Ophelia about hearing you out."

Seth looked at her, "She said no, didn't she?"

"She said she couldn't." Shelby touched his arm; "She's still so hurt over everything. She's confused; doesn't know what to do about her feelings. Right now, I don't think she would hear what you have to say if she sat down with you. Her solution is not to deal with it and until she does, I don't think you will get through to her." Shelby looked at him concerned. She knew her brother was just as hurt if not more because he caused their situation.

Seth looked down, "What am I going to do? There is no getting over her. I hate my work, I hate everything right now." Seth sat down on one of the deck benches.

"She's not getting over you either. I've never seen her like this. She's either sad or in business mode right now. She spent a little time with the boys. I thought that would help since it's hard to be sad around them. Their happiness usually can lift your mood; but even Owen asked her if she was still sad and if the glue was starting to work." Shelby pouted her lip, "My boys miss having you both together." Shelby touched Seth's shoulder, "Give it some more time."

Ophelia opened for business on Monday, February 5th. Her legal secretary worked 8-5 answering phones and helping with marketing. At the completion of her second workweek she had six clients, definitely a great start, and an appointment scheduled for the following Tuesday with a potential client for franchising documentation for twelve states which would keep her busy. Ophelia was excited for the meeting and hoped she and the client would want to work together.

Seth was slinging drinks behind the bar when Addison and Marren took stools at the bar rail.

Seth smiled, "Hello ladies, what can I get for you?"

Seth's smile was polite even though he felt a bit awkward with Ophelia's friends. He didn't know if they knew exactly what a complete ass he had been. Putting napkins in front of them they give him their drink order. This wasn't the first time the FBI friends had been in since their break up, but they usually sat at a table allowing him to keep his distance but still say hello. Addison had originally shared on a previous visit that she was back in town on a case with the

Mobile office but tonight they were celebrating she was permanently assigned. The ladies asked for a food menu to add snacks to the celebration.

"How are you doing Seth?" Addison knew that he and Ophelia had taken their break up very hard, though Ophelia didn't share all the details.

"I'm doing alright. How are you? Congratulations on the new assignment."

"Thank you. We are celebrating some changes, not only my staying put but some of the agents and staff are moving around so we will get fresh blood." Addison looked up at Seth, "They asked her to come back but she declined. They offered her a supervisor position in Mobile or a choice of a few other cities but she still said no. Looks like she likes it where she is."

Seth pushed his lips together and nodded. He didn't want to talk about Ophelia with her friends. He knew she and Addison were close but he also knew Ophelia was private about things. He got busy with other customers and left the women to enjoy themselves. Seth's mind raced, all that he did, all the hurt that he caused, and she would have only been in DC less than three months. The news made him feel worse. He had devastated his life, lost his love, and for what? For Ophelia to get the offer she wanted three months after he pushed her away at Thanksgiving.

The bar started filling up with dinner customers and to the girls delight, a handsome, polished man sat down one seat away from Addison and Marren. He was dressed in a plaid dress shirt and nice slacks. He looked like he had some money in his pocket but his attractive face was what Addison took notice of first. She guessed him to be mid to late 30's. He had a young face but the way he presented himself and dressed made her believe he was older and accomplished.

She and Marren continued to talk about work and their plans for the weekend when new drinks appeared in front of them.

Seth said, "This gentlemen wanted to buy both of you a drink." Seth gestured to the handsome stranger.

Brogan McCaffrey was not a stranger to Seth. He had been coming in to the bar for about three weeks. He was renting the apartment above Pinzone's Italian Downtown while he was doing business in Orange Beach.

"Thank you," Addison smiled at Brogan.

Seth quickly introduced them.

Addison extended her hand, "Nice to meet you." Marren extended her hand after Brogan was finished shaking Addison's.

"My pleasure." Brogan smiled picking up his beer taking a drink.

"Are you new in town? You don't have the southern accent." Addison noticed.

"I am. I've been in Fairhope about three weeks now. I'm here for work. You don't have the southern accent either. Are you a transplant? Or visiting?"

"I'm here for work, well actually I just received a permanent transfer. So this is my new home. I'm thrilled. I love it here." Addison gestured to Marren, "Marren is a permanent resident." She looked at Marren, "A couple years now, right?" Addison asked.

Marren smiled, "Yes. I live in Mobile actually."

"What kind of work do you do?" Brogan asked.

Addison smiled, "What kind of work do you do?"

Brogan chuckled, "I'm here opening a restaurant in Orange Beach. It's the second and we are getting ready to Franchise. My business partner is more familiar with the area and recommended I stay in Fairhope; so here I am."

"We are FBI working out of the Mobile field office." Addison stated.

Brogan smiled with a nod, "I had dinner with my attorney last night, she is former FBI. Do you know Ophelia Griffin?"

"She is a good friend of ours. If she is your attorney, you are in good hands." Addison smiled and looked to see if Seth was listening. He didn't look over but was within hearing distance.

"I know I am. She's brilliant, she puts my New York attorney to shame." Brogan chuckled again. "I know the former Attorney General, he couldn't say enough about her. I was surprised she left the Bureau with such a promising career; not that I'm upset. Her opening her own practice is to my benefit for sure."

Addison nodded, "She loves the law and her hours are better than ours." Addison gestured to her and Marren.

Marren added, "Not to mention the pay," with a laugh.

Both women nodded in agreement happy for their friend.

"It's important to love what you do. Do you love what you do?" Brogan asked Addison.

"I do for the most part. I love the investigation work. Do you like the restaurant business?"

"Love it. Love growing a new business. I'm what you would call a serial entrepreneur. I get very involved with new projects, grow them and sell them moving on to the next." Brogan offered.

The conversation went on for another hour with everyone eating and enjoying another drink. Brogan was getting ready to leave but asked a few more questions about Ophelia.

Brogan smiled, "I enjoyed having conversation with my meal. It's been pretty quiet for me besides work. Makes me miss hanging out with friends. Thank you."

"Well, you should consider us friends. Come hang out anytime. We frequent here and Fly Bar." Marren offered.

"I'll take you up on it. Maybe Ophelia will join us. I've been giving her some grief that she's working too much. I'm getting emails from her sometimes at 2am. She seems all business all the time. Don't get me wrong, I love that she's on top of things, but she needs to have a little fun. I don't know her personal story but she seems, I don't know?"

Addison smiled, "She's pretty private about her personal story so I'll leave that up to her to share. Ophelia is business and when you have a business relationship with her she keeps it professional all the time. I'm sure you already know that from the A.G.?"

"I do. But we are working together frequently and I'm hoping we can not only work together but also be friends. Ophelia is cool. Definitely someone that I could see wanting to hang out with. She's a perfect mix of sarcasm and wit."

Brogan wanted the scoop on what was up with Ophelia's personal life. Not because he would date his attorney but because many times she looked sad. He was fond of her.

Addison looked up to see Seth give a sideways glance at Brogan.

Addison smiled, "Sarcasm and wit quickly turns to sassy if you're not careful," Addison giggled. Returning to a serious face, "She's also pretty tight lipped when it comes to her personal life. I have to keep the girl code." Addison gave a little laugh, "We are all good at keeping secrets, comes with the job."

Brogan smiled, "Fair enough. The more time we spend together, I'm sure I'll get to know her better."

"Of course." Addison confirmed.

Seth was upset. Was she dating? It didn't sound like a date and he knew her. She wouldn't date a client, but dinner? Was Brogan interested in her? Of course he was, what man wouldn't be? Seth asked the other bartender to cover for him and walked in his office, closing the door behind him.

"Hello."

"Is she dating?" Seth asked his sister as soon as Shelby picked up the phone.

"Hi Seth. How are you?"

"Is Ophelia dating?" Seth didn't have time to make small talk.

"No. I'm not aware of her dating. Actually, no she's not dating. I think if anything she hates men." Shelby said with a huff.

"Are you sure?" Seth wanted confirmation. "You told me to lay off the flowers and such. I did and one of her clients was in here tonight talking about how he was out to dinner with her."

Shelby laughed, "Ophelia had dinner with a client? Oh my God. That is unheard of, an attorney having dinner with a client. I'm calling the Fairhope newspaper for the complete lack of moral code."

"Shut up. I'm being serious. The guy had all these nice things to say about her. He's I don't know; you would think he's handsome. A business man with means."

"Oh so a handsome business man that can afford her hourly rate has hired a beautiful, genius attorney to represent him; and thinks highly of her. Hmmm, sounds like they are getting ready to walk down the aisle. Jesus Seth, she's an attorney and more professional than…" Shelby couldn't think of the words. "Let's just say, I doubt she's letting her client anywhere near her personal life. Go back to work. I love you."

Seth sighed, "I love you, too."

CHAPTER 20

"**T**hank you for holding the tables. I know Friday nights are busy for you." Michelle hugged Seth.

"Of course. It's your Birthday! Happy Birthday. The waitress is going to take care of you tonight. I don't think I'm going to stick around. I doubt Ophelia will show up if she knows I'm here. She hasn't stepped in the bar since December."

Seth couldn't believe it had been two months since the Christmas party disaster. And honestly he didn't know if he was up to seeing her especially after not being convinced she wasn't dating. Wednesday's conversation he overheard had put him in a tailspin.

"She promised me she would come to my birthday party." Michelle stood near the dance floor talking to Seth while Ken played on the large stage on the back patio. "If Ophelia promises, she will be here no matter if you are here or not. So, yes you will stay, plus it gets you in front of her." Michelle smiled.

"She doesn't want to be in front of me." Seth took a drink of his beer, watching Ken play the guitar and sing. Michelle's husband was an excellent musician and agreed to play all of her favorite songs for her birthday.

"Maybe she doesn't know that she really does want to be in front of you? She's been working non-stop. I can't help but think she's trying to avoid dealing with missing you." Michelle smiled, "I'm hoping my party opens the door."

Seth smiled, "Thanks Michelle but just enjoy your birthday. I don't want you to worry about me. I'll figure something out."

Friends joining the party on the patio interrupted Michelle and Seth. Michelle hugged everyone and accepted birthday wishes. Soon Seth got lost in conversation with a few guys that stood around a nearby table. The party was well underway when Ophelia joined the group.

Ophelia walked to the edge of the back patio. She noticed Seth had been busy installing heaters and a retractable ceiling so he could use the back patio during the winter months. The place looked great. She took a deep breath and entered the patio carrying a pink gift-wrapped box with a beautiful bow. Instead of spotting Michelle, Ophelia saw Seth talking to friends and avoided eye contact, looking in a different direction. She knew he would be at the party, but Michelle had made her promise to come, telling her that with so many people at the bar, Seth would be too busy to pay her any mind. Michelle squealed when she spotted Ophelia, wrapping her arms around her in a big hug.

"I've missed you girl. You are working too hard." Michelle squeezed Ophelia tight.

"Happy Birthday. Looks like you are loved." Ophelia smiled, looking at the balloons and streamers.

"Ken makes a big deal about my birthday, and I love it." She smiled.

Several friends joined Ophelia and Michelle's conversation. Topics from clothes, kids, and dating were covered and when the conversation turned to sex; the laughter took over. Ophelia not only laughed but also felt her cheeks turn pink at several comments the women made.

"Did ya'll see the new comber in town Brogan McCaffrey?" One of Michelle's single girlfriends, Carrie, asked.

Michelle nodded, "Nice guy. He comes in here for dinner pretty often. Brogan is staying in Fairhope for work."

"Well that man caused a flood in my lady basement. He's beyond handsome." Said the single friend.

Michelle laughed out loud while Ophelia almost choked on her beer that was delivered seconds before.

"Dear Lord, Carrie you are so colorful." Michelle rolled her eyes with laughter.

Ophelia blushed and was uncomfortable. Brogan was her client and though she knew he was handsome, she didn't think of him in any way other than as a business acquaintance.

"All I know is, he deserves a little attention and I'm just the girl to give it to him." Carrie smiled.

While Michelle told Carrie to cool her jets, Ophelia made her way to the bathroom. She started thinking of when a good time would be to leave. Ophelia knew that she could sneak out when Michelle got busy with her other guests or when the dancing started. Returning from the bathroom, she watched Michelle and the group of girls on the dance floor. Michelle was looking for Ophelia and walked over, taking her by the hand and encouraging Ophelia to join in the fun. Ophelia danced two songs with Michelle and the music changed to a slow song. Ken stepped off the stage and took Michelle in his arms. He continued to sing while he swayed with Michelle to the music. Ophelia smiled and turned to leave the dance floor but Seth stood in her way.

Seth gently took Ophelia in his arms and to his surprise, she didn't make a fuss. He figured she didn't want to embarrass him or cause anyone to take notice. Her body was soft against him. He took her hand in his and with this other hand he found the middle of her back. Ophelia placed her free hand on his shoulder and her face was hidden in his collarbone.

Seth looked down taking in the smell of her hair, "I miss you so much." He spoke in her ear.

Ophelia's voice was soft and without anger, "I don't want to talk."

"Ok. No talking. I'll just hold on to you for however long you let me."

One song turned in to two with Seth never wanting the music to end. His lips touched her forehead and he brought her hand that he was holding to his chest, releasing it. Ophelia opened her hand, touching his chest while they swayed. Seth was happy that she let him pull her in close with both his arms wrapped around her.

When the song ended, Ophelia backed up, raising her eyes for just a moment to look at Seth, "Thank you."

She walked to the table where her beer and purse were placed before the dancing started again. It wasn't long and the dance floor was crowded allowing enough cover for Ophelia to sneak out. She walked past the dining tables in the front of the bar and out of the main entrance. Tears spilled out of her eyes the moment her feet hit the sidewalk. The two blocks of cool night air did nothing to stop the damn from bursting; she couldn't turn the tears off. Seeing Seth, holding him close, was too much. She ached for him, feeling broken and lonely she turned the corner spotting her car and Seth standing waiting for her.

Seth watched her leave the patio, exiting through the front door, knowing she was upset. He walked out the back door and took the opposite block. He knew where her car was parked so he waited. Ophelia wiped her tears when she approached but it did no good, they continued.

Seth looked at her lovingly, "I'll take you home, you shouldn't drive upset." He put out his hand for her keys.

Ophelia continued to cry and without saying anything handed him the keys. Seth opened the passenger door and she got in the car. She tried to wipe the tears away again and think of anything that would stop them from coming but it seemed that all the crying she had not allow herself to do over the last few months would not be held back.

The drive to Ophelia's bay house was quick. Seth parked, got out and went to her side of the car, opening the door. Ophelia said nothing, just walked up the stairs to her front door. Seth unlocked the door and opened it for her. He followed her inside and walked to the kitchen to get a bottle of water out of the refrigerator while she sat on the living room couch. Seth stopped in the bathroom to get a box of Kleenex before he joined her on the couch. Ophelia took a Kleenex and a drink of the water he offered. Neither of them had turned a light on but with the moonlight coming in the room, Seth could see the tears still sliding down Ophelia's cheeks. He put his arm around her and she turned, pressing her face in his chest. She thought to herself that she wanted him to take the hurt away, make everything the way it was when they were together and happy. Tears continued to fall while she clung to him. Seth held her, and ran his hand over her hair. His lips kissed her forehead numerous times. He felt miserable that he had made her this unhappy, he was the cause of her tears and heartache and he could barely stand himself. Seth leaned back on the couch, resting Ophelia to his chest and letting her cry.

He continued to try and comfort her, holding her and stroking her hair but stayed as silent as he could only saying, "I love you, baby."

Seth wasn't sure what else to say and she had already told him she didn't want to talk. What he needed now was for her to tell him what to do, what she wanted. Seeing her this way, if she wanted him to leave her alone, he would do whatever it took so she wasn't miserable. Seth held her until early morning after letting her cry herself to sleep.

Ophelia woke covered in a blanket resting on a pillow on her couch. Seth was gone but he left a note on the coffee table.

Ophelia -
I love you.
I will do anything to stop you from hurting.
Tell me what to do and I'll do it.
Seth

Seth stood in his parent's kitchen at 6am making coffee.

"Where did you come from?" Mom asked pulling a cup out of the cabinet.

Seth looked at her, "I walked here from Ophelia's. She was at Michelle's birthday party and I upset her. I drove her home."

"How and why did you upset her?" Mom raised an eyebrow looking at him with an unpleasant scowl.

"I danced with her and that seemed fine at first but when I watched her I knew she was upset. She walked to her car crying and I couldn't let her drive like that. We didn't talk. She just cried." Seth looked at his mom, "I have hurt her so much, broken her heart. I should have gone with her to D.C., put her first. I should have taken care of her, made sure nothing hurt her instead of being the one that has caused all this pain. She's miserable, what do I do?" Seth's eyes were filled with tears.

"I don't know sweetheart. Maybe all the tears last night will make the way for something else. I don't think she's let herself cry. Ophelia bottles everything up and gets busy until she can't hold it in anymore." Mom gave him a thoughtful look and touched his cheek.

"Do I let her go? I don't want her unhappy. I love her so much, I can't have her hurting like this."

Mom smiled gently, "Don't do anything. Don't give up yet. Wait and see." She poured herself a cup of coffee.

CHAPTER 21

O phelia was stood talking to her receptionist when Mom Corrigan walked in her law office on Tuesday afternoon. It had been two weeks since her son showed up at her house after the night of Michelle's party. Neither Seth nor Ophelia had made a move to talk to each other and Ophelia had missed another Sunday dinner.

Ophelia's face lit up, "Hi Mom Corrigan, this is a nice surprise."

"Hi Sweetheart." Mom Corrigan hugged her, "I want to talk to you. Do you have time?"

"Of course. Do you want something to drink?" Ophelia offered while she led Mom Corrigan to her office.

"I'm just fine." Mom Corrigan smiled setting her purse on Ophelia's desk. She turned to her and hugged her again; "You know how much I love you, right?"

Ophelia looked concerned, "Yes ma'am. Are you ok? Is Dad?"

"Yes, yes everyone is fine." Mom Corrigan sat down.

Ophelia did the same, sitting in the guest chair next to her.

Mom Corrigan looked at Ophelia with a serious and concerned face, "I've done my best to stay out of your business, leaving you and Seth to do what you need to but something needs to change." Mom took a breath giving both of them a moment. "Sweetheart, I haven't seen you really smile in months. You can't go on like this. You are staying away from the family and I won't have it."

Ophelia looked down, "I don't want to make anyone uncomfortable."

Mom lifted Ophelia's chin with her fingers, "Ophelia, not having you with us is uncomfortable. You are part of our family. You have been since you were 5 years old. I will not have you stay away. Dad and I love you like you are our own and it is hurting us that you are not with us. Your parents were our very best friends. Your Momma and Daddy treated my children like they were theirs. That's how we were and how it will always be. You are mine, and you will be at the house with our family."

Ophelia looked like a young girl who was scolded, "Yes ma'am". Tears filled her eyes.

"Now you have a choice to make. You get over Seth, move on and find happiness, or you give him a second chance and find happiness. Either way, I want to see you happy." Mom searched Ophelia's face.

"What do I do? I can't get over him but I'm scared to give us another chance." Ophelia asked.

"Honey, do you love him?"

"So much it hurts."

Mom looked at her concerned, "I don't think you walk away from love."

Ophelia looked down with a nod.

"Think on it. But whatever you decide, you are part of this family. You will be at Sunday dinner. You and Seth will just have to not talk or figure out how to deal with each other; whatever, but I won't have you stay away. Understood?" Mom gave her a gentle smile.

"Yes ma'am." Ophelia nodded.

"Alright. Shelby will be here on Thursday to watch the

Leprechaun Bike Parade. We plan to sit on this corner and watch those silly men walk by. You will join in the fun. On Sunday we will have dinner as a family." Mom paused taking Ophelia's hands, "I love you, my sweet girl."

Mom let her hands go and touched her face, wiping tears that had escaped Ophelia's eyes. They both stood and hugged each other.

"I love you. I'm missing you and Dad." Ophelia squeezed her tight.

Seth watched his mother walk in the bar and sit down in front of him on a barstool.

"Come sit with your Momma." She gave him a smile.

Seth poured them both some sweet tea and sat next to her. They both took a drink of the tea. Seth braced himself for what was coming; it was rare she would come to see him at work.

"I just left Ophelia. She will be at Sunday dinner. You will be at Sunday dinner. You'll both just have to figure out how to be around each other."

Seth shook his head, "That's not a good idea. I don't want her upset."

Mom shook her head back at him, "Seth, she is part of this family, just like you are. No matter if the two of you work out or don't, that girl will always be part of this family. You will have to figure out a way to live with whatever she decides, just like she will have to live with it. Now this is not up for discussion. We will have dinner as a family on Sunday. Understood?"

Seth looked at his mom, "Yes ma'am."

CHAPTER 22

McSharry's Irish Pub sponsored the St. Patrick's Day Leprechaun Bicycle Parade. The Pub offered prizes for best Leprechaun, Best Beard, and Best Irish Jig. Seth, Dad Corrigan and Michael dressed accordingly for the ride. In full leprechaun attire they rode decorated bicycles down the streets of downtown Fairhope. Spectators lined both sides of Fairhope Avenue to enjoy the ride that was kicking off the St. Patrick's Day celebration weekend. Mom Corrigan, Ophelia, and Shelby sat in outdoor chairs curbside in front of Ophelia's building. The three enjoyed the show, laughing hysterically at all the men dressed in very elaborate green suits with orange hair and beards. Seth made eye contact with Ophelia when he rode by and they shared a big smile and laugh. The festivities wrapped up in front of McSharry's with the announcing of the prizewinners. Ophelia said her goodbyes to Mom Corrigan and Shelby. She excused herself, heading back to her office to finish for the night.

It wasn't long and she heard her receptionist, Mary say, "Ophelia, you have a leprechaun here to see you."

Seth looked at Ophelia's receptionist, "Really?"

"How many times will I get the opportunity to say that?" Mary laughed.

Ophelia was laughing a little walking around the corner motioning for Seth to come in her office. "Hi. You look very Irish."

Ophelia giggled.

Seth smirked, "Well, I didn't win."

Ophelia nodded, "There was some fierce competition. I wouldn't take it too hard."

Seth pulled off the hat, wig and beard so he could talk to her without her laughing at him. He ran his fingers through his hair so he looked as normal as possible dressed in a green suit.

Ophelia watched him, noticing that he was nervous, "Can I get you something to drink?"

Seth shook his head, "Thank you but no, I'm fine. Shelby told me that you are watching the boys on Saturday night instead of coming out for St. Patrick's Day."

Ophelia smiled with a nod, "Owen and Jake are spending the night. I promised we would bake cookies and read stories."

Seth looked at her with concern, "If you want to come out, Shelby can get a sitter. I promise I won't make you uncomfortable. Everyone's going to be at the bar, it will be fun. I don't want you to miss out on anything because of me."

"I'm not staying home with the boys because of you. I miss the boys and haven't been able to spend much time with them. I'll have them to myself and it gives Shelby and Mike a night out."

Ophelia's face showed her genuine delight in the idea of having Jake and Owen for the night. Seth felt relieved seeing that Ophelia was happy to be spending the evening with his nephews.

"Momma said she had a visit with you. She had a visit with me too."

Ophelia gave him a half smile, "I guess you'll be at Sunday dinner?"

Seth slowly nodded, "Are you going to be ok with that?"

Ophelia's head nodded, "Yes. I think I have my faucet under control. Thank you for driving me home when I was so upset." Ophelia looked down a little embarrassed.

"Of course. I'm sorry I caused those tears." Seth waited to see her reaction.

"I had been putting them off. It wasn't because of the dancing." Ophelia looked up nervous, "I'll be on my best behavior Sunday. I have the water works under control." She gave a slight smile wanting the conversation to be over. Her office was not the place for anything more than what they had already said.

She walked closer to the door, "I know you have some Leprechaun buddies waiting for you."

Seth nodded, walking closer to the door. He turned to stand in front of her. With gentle fingers he touched the wisps of hair that framed her face. He took a chance asking, "Will you have a cup of coffee with me or a glass of wine, sometime? Hear me out?"

Ophelia's eyes met his, "Yes."

Shelby dropped off the boys, giving them instructions to be on their best behavior.

Ophelia rolled her eyes, "They will be just fine. Go have fun. The boys and I have our own St. Patrick's Day plans."

The night with the boys was fun with time flying by quickly. Both little boys fell asleep watching TV by 9pm. Ophelia carried the boys to bed in the downstairs spare bedroom. Her living room was a littering of Nerf guns, bullets, and targets, soda cans and popcorn bowls to clean up. The kitchen was just as messy with icing and cookie making to be put away. Ophelia had prepared Irish stew to take for Sunday dinner at the Corrigan's along with soda bread. With Owen and Jake tucked in bed and the night still early for her, she cleaned up the living room and was almost done putting food away in the kitchen when she heard knocking at the door. Ophelia was dressed in a green t-shirt and shamrock pajama pants, not expecting company. Her hair was in a ponytail and she smoothed it and took a quick once over look at herself in the foyer mirror after seeing that Seth was doing the knocking.

Ophelia opened the door, "Hey, everything ok?"

"Yeah. I figured the boys were sleeping. I brought coffee and wine." He showed her both.

Ophelia held the door open for him, "Come in. I'm putting food away in the kitchen."

Seth walked in the door then followed her to the kitchen.

"Would you rather have a beer? After all it's St. Patrick's Day." Ophelia opened the refrigerator.

"I guess we should probably stick with tradition." Seth smiled nervously. He opened the beers Ophelia placed on the counter, "How were the boys?"

"Fun. We had a big night. They fell asleep watching TV. I have them in the guest bedroom." Ophelia smiled sipping her beer. She continued to put cookies in the container. "The cookie decorating was messy and I'm not sure the cookies are recognizable but they should taste good." She gave a little giggle.

"What smells good?" Seth sipped his beer.

"Irish stew and soda bread. My Momma's recipes. I'm bringing them to dinner tomorrow. Do you want to taste the stew?"

"I remember your Momma's stew, it was always so good." Seth smiled.

Ophelia spooned a small amount in a bowl, "Try it and make sure I got it right. I think I did." She handed the stew and a spoon to Seth.

He blew on a spoonful of stew to cool it slightly before taking a mouthful. He started to nod and smiled after swallowing, "It's perfect. Have you ever made it before?"

Ophelia shook her head, "No. She always did. I was too busy going out having fun on St. Patrick's Day to pay attention to what she was cooking. I remember her making it the night before saying it was always better the next day. Your mom told me it was their tradition to have her stew so I thought I'd try it."

"It's delicious." Seth finished eating what she had served in the bowl. He watched her put the last of the food away and pick up her beer.

Ophelia stood a couple feet away from him, "How was tonight? I'm sure the bar is still busy?"

"It's packed but I had plenty of staff working to handle it. Looks like you had some gun shooting going on tonight?" Seth smirked. He noticed the Nerf guns and targets set out in the living room.

"The boys are good with the targets and nobody lost an eye when they went all out assault, so I think it was a good night." She laughed.

"Well they do have guidance from a Quantico trained gun slinger. I would expect Owen and Jake to be very good with the targets. And they are good with moving targets, I've been shot many times." He laughed. Seth's face got a little serious, "Any book reading?"

"We read one book. Actually read the book since their questions were asked during the cookie decorating." Ophelia took another drink of her beer.

"They were suppose to go easy on the questions." Seth looked at her with loving eyes.

"Owen told me you asked them to go easy on me. Not to ask so many questions. They were sweet and very curious if the glue they bought me at Christmas has finally fixed my heart."

Seth nodded with a hmm sound, "Doesn't sound like they went

easy on you."

Ophelia smiled, "They think I have all the answers so I don't suppose they would." She took another drink of her beer.

Seth took a drink of his beer. His face was serious and he felt nervous and a bit afraid of what the outcome of the conversation that he needed to have with Ophelia would be.

"I made some big mistakes. Mistakes I will never make again." Seth paused looking at her. "I hurt you and Saturday night, seeing that hurt; I didn't like myself. I don't ever want to cause you pain. I'm so sorry." Seth waited again looking at her for a moment. "I love you so much. I was so selfish, wanting you to do what I wanted. I should have put you first, put us first. I know you have been offered a promotion with the FBI. Addison told me they offered you the Mobile field house or several other cities to get you to return. I spoke to the school and I can take a year leave without losing my seniority. I will follow you wherever you want to go." Seth moved a little closer to her, "We can live anywhere you want and if you want to stay there permanently, I can tell the school I won't be back." Seth paused again watching her face; he could see some of the tension relax on her forehead, "If you could love me again, I promise I will be the man that I should have always been. All that matters is that I'm with you."

Ophelia's eyes were wide looking at him, "Seth, I don't have to love you again. I never stopped loving you. I have already declined the FBI's offers; I'm home. My law practice is growing and I'm enjoying it. I don't want to be away from you or our family; I never did." Ophelia hesitated, "I just wanted us to be partners, equals; making decisions for our life together. I love you. All the hurt and tears, I missed you so much. I miss us."

Seth reached for Ophelia and holding the nape of her neck he pulled her to him. The embrace was tight against him.

He spoke into her hair, "Can I come home to you?"

Ophelia clenched the sides of Seth's shirt, "Promise we will never be apart."

Seth moved back slightly to look in her eyes, "Never apart. I love you."

"I love you." Her eyes matched the words she spoke; the spark he longed for was back.

Seth's lips were forceful and hard on Ophelia's mouth, giving her a brusied feeling, but it was a good hurt.

Her body melted onto him and she whispered, "Take me upstairs."

Seth didn't stop kissing her as they slowly made their way to the staircase.

"Wait," Ophelia broke the kiss, "I need to check on the boys." She walked to the spare bedroom and looked in on the two boys sleeping soundly. When she turned, Seth was watching her, his eyes had never left her. She approached and he took her hand, leading her up the stairs.

They stood at the edge of the bed removing each other's clothes. Seth's appreciation for her body was undeniable. He caressed every inch of her, kissed every place his hands touched until she shook with pleasure. His body moved over hers, laying her back on the bed. When he entered her, they both exhaled with desire and a relief of finally being where they should be. Satisfied quickly, they relaxed in each other's arms. Ophelia rested her cheek to Seth's chest with his arm wrapped around her.

She smiled, "I fit perfectly right here."

"Yes you do. You have always fit perfectly with me." Seth smiled pulling her a little closer.

It was a long time before they moved, just enjoying being in each other's arms.

"I'm going to get some water and check on the boys." Seth offered.

When he returned Ophelia was sitting on the small couch wrapped in a blanket looking out the French doors. The moon on the water was romantic and beautiful.

"The boys haven't moved." Seth handed Ophelia an opened bottle of water.

She took a sip and handed it back to him. Seth placed the water on the nightstand and joined Ophelia on the couch.

"You were right, the couch is perfect here."

She smiled, "I love to watch the water."

Ophelia moved to him, opening the blanket to rest her body against his.

Seth stroked her hair and held her, "You're everything to me. I'm going to make you happy for the rest of our lives. I promise you."

Ophelia lifted her face to kiss him. Their lips, soft and gentle, caressed each other, their tongues tangled, and a sweet moan left Ophelia. Seth shifted, lowering himself with his knees on the floor in front of the couch. He ran his hands along the top of her thighs and looked up at her.

"I never knew I could love anyone the way I love you. My life doesn't work without you." He took her hands, "Ophelia, will you spend your life with me? Do me the honor of being my wife?" Seth held the ring in his fingers.

Ophelia nodded her head and a beaming smile lit up her face. "Yes, I will be your wife."Seth slipped the ring on her finger and his lips kissed the hand that he placed the ring on. He moved between her legs, kissing his way up to her mouth. Lifting her he turned, sitting on the couch with Ophelia now straddled on top of him.

"I love you every minute." His lips were wild kissing and tugging on hers with soft teeth. Ophelia lifted her body, guiding Seth deep inside her.

Ophelia's head fell back as she felt him thick and deep. Her head slowly returned to look at him, "I love you, Seth." She kissed him with soft gentle lips, "I belong with you. I'm lost without you."

Her hips rotated, pushed and pulled. Seth held on to her hips, letting her take what she wanted from him without leading or driving the speed. She took her time at first, enjoying a slow chase to the finish line. He pulled her hard to him when he felt her tighten, helping her over the edge.

Ophelia came down from the high, her face in the crook of his neck, "You feel so good. You make me feel so good."

Seth smiled and lifted them off the couch, "That was all you, baby." He walked to the bed, placing her on her back to have his way with her.

"Uncle Seth!" Both boys yelled, racing in the kitchen and grabbing Seth's legs to hug him.

"Good morning gentlemen. Help me out with these beignets." Seth ushered them to the sink to wash their hands. "You will need to put the powdered sugar on them."

The boys sat on the stools at the island and sprinkled the French donuts with sugar when Seth placed them on the plate.

"Where is Aunt Ophelia?" Owen asked.

"We are letting her sleep a little longer." Seth smiled.

Jake asked, "But we can wake her up, right?"

Seth nodded, "Yes, you both can wake her up when breakfast is ready."

Breakfast was ready and the boys started racing up the stairs, "Aunt Ophelia wake up, Uncle Seth is here. We made beignets!"

Ophelia was awake under the covers, dressed in her pajamas. When the boys approached the edge of the bed she reached for them pulling them to her and tickled them.

"Did you boys have good dreams last night?"

"Yes, Aunt Ophelia! I dreamed about cookies." Owen said.

Jake followed, "I dreamed about pulling up the crab traps."

"Sounds like you two had good dreams." Ophelia kissed their noses.

"Uncle Seth is here. Did you know he was making all of us breakfast?" Owen asked.

"We are lucky. Your Uncle Seth makes the best beignets." Ophelia stood taking each boys hand, "Let's have breakfast."

Owen and Jake raced up the stairs of the Corrigan Bay House, "Gram, Gramp, Momma, Dad we are home!"

The boys swung the door open, running in the house. Seth and Ophelia walked in after them carrying stew, bread and cookies. Mom Corrigan greeted them at the door.

She was surprised, "Did you drive together?"

Ophelia smiled, "Yes, we did."

She kissed Mom on the cheek and headed to the kitchen. Mom looked at Seth with a questioning look.

"What?" Seth smiled, "My fiancé and I wanted to drive together. What's the big deal?" With a bigger smile he shrugged his shoulders.

Mom Corrigan put her hand on his face, "I'm so happy."

"I am too." Seth couldn't help the smile that wouldn't go away.

After lunch the family sat on the screened in back deck enjoying the view and sweet tea.

Shelby, holding Ophelia's ring finger said, "It's beautiful and looks like you."

"I know. I love it." Ophelia smiled, holding it up for the sunlight to make it sparkle that much more.

Seth enjoyed listening and watching Ophelia talk about her ring and getting married.

"When is the wedding and where? Can I pick out my dress?" Shelby started asking questions.

"Your brother and I haven't talked about it yet. Don't start making plans for us. Yes, you can pick out your dress; nothing too fancy." Ophelia smiled and hugged Shelby.

The newly engaged couple said good-bye to everyone and headed home at 4pm when Shelby and her family left for Birmingham. Seth held Ophelia's hand, opening the passenger door of his car.

She touched his face and kissed him, "Will you go see my Momma with me?"

"Of course."

They arrived at Homestead Village and found Ophelia's mom sitting in her room looking out the window.

Ophelia took the lead walking in the room, "Mrs. Griffin, are you up for some company?"

Ophelia's mother looked at her but didn't say anything.

Ophelia walked in with Seth following her. "It's a beautiful day, do want to sit on the porch?"

Ellie Griffin stood, "That would be nice."

Ophelia smiled, "This is Seth."

Ophelia's mom took the arm that Seth offered. The three sat on the porch for a long time with Ophelia and her mom talking about flowers and food that they liked to eat.

"It's so nice of you to visit with me. But I'm waiting for my family; I should get back to my room." Ellie stated.

Ophelia gently smiled, "Of course. I'll take you in. I wanted to show you my engagement ring. Seth asked me to marry him."

Ophelia held out her hand showing off her ring.

"Sugar, the ring is beautiful. Almost as beautiful as your smile." Ellie touched Ophelia's chin, which was a rare occasion.

Ophelia's eyes filled with tears, "Thank you."

Seth could see Ophelia's face and stepped in, "Mrs. Griffin, I would love to escort you in." Seth offered her his arm.

Ophelia waited on the porch for Seth to return.

When he did he wrapped his arm around her, "She's all set. I let the nurse know she was in her room."

Ophelia rested her head on his chest, "Thank you. I just wanted..." Ophelia stopped talking.

"You wanted your Momma to know what a lucky man I am. I understand that. Somewhere locked inside, she knows. I believe that." Seth kissed Ophelia on the top of her head.

CHAPTER 23

"Three weeks? You are getting married in three weeks? How will I ever find a dress and get a bachelorette party and everything ready in three weeks?!" Shelby protested holding the phone to her ear while she made breakfast for the boys.

Ophelia pulled paperwork together for her meeting, holding the phone under her chin, "That is what I want and your brother agrees. It's going to be a small wedding and reception at the bay house. I don't need a bachelorette party and you can wear a pretty summer dress."

"Of course you need a bachelorette party! Any color in particular for the dress?" Shelby asked.

"The flowers are magnolias, white roses and blue hydrangeas so any color dress is going to be fine. Make sure Mike's tie goes with your dress. I have a meeting. Love you." Ophelia said.

"Love you." Shelby hung up and called her brother.

"Why a small wedding in three weeks?"

"Good Morning, how are you?" Seth asked.

"Good Morning. Spill it."

Seth laughed at her response. "We don't want to wait. We want to start our life together as husband and wife, right now. Ophelia can have whatever she wants; she wants a small wedding with close friends and our family. That's all we need. Relax, we are both happy." Seth smiled at the phone.

"Are you sure she doesn't want the reception at the Grand Hotel?" Shelby asked.

"I'm 100%. She's picked everything that she wants. Remember this is Ophelia; she's not you. Miss Flashy." Seth laughed.

"Ok. I just want everything perfect for her. Is she going to ask Daddy to walk her down the aisle?" Shelby asked.

"Yes she is. I'm going to take her to see her Momma in her wedding dress between the wedding and the reception." Seth confirmed.

Ophelia knocked on the door and waited. Mom Corrigan opened the door, "Hi Sweetheart, don't wait outside, just walk in."

Ophelia nodded and kissed Mom's cheek, "Hi Mom. How are you today?"

"I'm good. Are you on your lunch?"

Ophelia nodded, "I was hoping to catch Dad."

"He's out back on the dock. What can I fix you to eat?"

"I'm not hungry. But thank you."

"Take you and Dad some tea."

Ophelia followed mom into the kitchen and poured two glasses of sweet tea to take to the dock.

"Hey Sweet Girl." Dad smiled at Ophelia as she approached.

"Hi Dad. Mom sent you some sweet tea."

Dad took the glass she offered, putting it to his lips. He took a drink, "Thank you. Lunch time?"

Ophelia smiled, "Yes kind of. I have a break and was hoping to talk to you."

Dad secured the fishing rod, "You can always talk to me."

Ophelia smiled and her eyes got a little teary, "Will you walk me down the aisle and give me away?"

Dad smiled pulling her in his arms for a warm loving hug, "I was hoping you would ask me. It would be my pleasure to help your Daddy out on your wedding day."

Ophelia wrapped her arms around him, "Thank you."

Dad patted her back, "You are going to be a beautiful bride. Your Daddy will be watching."

Ophelia smiled and nodded.

"My sister called worried you might want the reception at the Grand Hotel." Seth spoke as he ran his fingers over Ophelia's naked back.

Ophelia turned her head to face him, resting her cheek on the pillow. "That feels nice. I want to have the reception here like we planned." She smiled.

"That's what I told her. Are you sure you want to keep everything small? You can have anything you want."

"I know; I can have anything. We are going to have a beautiful wedding with our friends and family. I don't have a need to invite people we don't see regularly or distant relatives. Are you ok with what we have planned?"

"I'm happy; I'm just double checking that you are. The only person I care about being there is you."

"Well, I'll be the one in the white dress." She smiled.

Seth moved closer, "I'm going to be the one waiting for you in the tux." He turned her over and took his place between her legs.

"I want to get to baby making." Ophelia smiled, "So, I'm double checking that you are ok with what we planned."

"You don't have to ask, baby making is my favorite part." Seth kissed her lips gently, moving his lips down her neck to her breasts and returning to her lips while he hooked her leg, pushing inside her.

Mom Corrigan walked in the spare bedroom at Ophelia and Seth's home. "My God, you are breath taking."

Ophelia turned in her wedding dress with a smile, "Don't cry. I'll cry and we will be a mess." Ophelia walked to Mom Corrigan and hugged her.

"I told her Seth is going to lose his mind." Shelby smiled.

Mom Corrigan smiled, "He is going to lose his mind." Mom Corrigan touched Ophelia's face, "Everyone is here. Ready?"

Ophelia nodded, "Ready."

"I'll send Dad in." Mom Corrigan kissed her cheek.

Dad Corrigan offered Ophelia his arm, "You look beautiful. I know your Daddy would ask you if you are truly happy so I'm asking. Are you happy?"

Ophelia smiled, "I couldn't be happier. He's my whole life and I know I'm his whole life."

Dad Corrigan kissed Ophelia's forehead, "Let's go see Seth."

Ophelia's smile lit up her face as she was escorted out the back door onto the deck. The walk was not far, only to the edge of the dock where Seth stood waiting with Mike by his side. Seth's eyes met Ophelia's. His smile let her know how beautiful she looked. His head tipped back just a little in awe of her.

He mouthed, "So beautiful."

Dad gave Ophelia's hand to Seth.

"Thanks, Dad." Seth nodded with a smile of gratitude.

Seth stood facing Ophelia, waiting for her to give Shelby her bouquet. When she turned and faced him, Seth took both her hands into his own.

He leaned in kissed her lips and cheek. "You are so beautiful. I'm so in love with you."

The minister cleared his throat, "It's not quite time for kissing, Seth."

The guests chuckled.

The ceremony concluded with the announcement of Seth and Ophelia as husband and wife. When Seth was instructed to kiss the bride, he kissed her slow and sweet to cheers and clapping.

He pulled his face away from the kiss, "You're mine forever."

Ophelia touched his face, "I am. And you're mine."

Seth and Ophelia greeted their guests receiving congratulations and best wishes. Champagne and appetizers were served while the caterers prepared dinner for everyone.

"This is a perfect time to go see your mom." Seth whispered in Ophelia's ear. "Let's go."

Ophelia nodded, taking Seth's hand.

Seth and Ophelia walked in to Homestead Village with the nursing staff greeting them with hugs and congratulations.

"She's in her room." The head nurse told Seth.

Ophelia walked in her mother's room finding her in a beautiful blue dress. "Hi, Mrs. Griffin."

Ellie Griffin turned away from the window, looked directly at Ophelia, "You are an angel. So beautiful."

"Thank you. It's my wedding day and I wanted to see you." Ophelia smiled.

Ophelia's mom walked to her, "You are so lovely. You look like me."

"I do." Ophelia looked at her mother and thought that she knew who she was. "This was yours." Ophelia touched the tiara that held her veil. "Daddy said you were the most beautiful bride."

Ellie smiled, "You are the most beautiful bride. Thank you for coming to see me."

"Can I hug you?" Ophelia asked.

"Of course, sweetheart." Ellie took Ophelia into a loving embrace that lasted longer than Ellie normally allowed.

Ophelia held Seth's hand walking to the car, "She knew me. I think she knew me."

Seth stopped taking Ophelia in his arms, "She knew you, baby. She did." He could feel Ophelia quake in a soft cry.

"Happy tears, I swear." Ophelia looked at Seth. "Let's go celebrate."

"You got it Mrs. Corrigan." Seth kissed her forehead then her lips. "I can't wait to dance with my wife."

"I can't wait to dance with my husband. And our nephews are looking forward to cake." They both laughed.

"Keep reading for a sneak peek at Fairhope Addison the next book in the Forever Fairhope Series!"

Ansley Prescott

FAIRHOPE ADDISON

FAIRHOPE ADDISON

CHAPTER 1

"**H**ey Addie, I was keeping Marren entertained while we waited for you and Ophelia. Beer or something stronger?"

Addison smiled, approaching the bar rail at Bone and Barrel Restaurant and Bar. "Hey Seth, I would love a beer. What's so entertaining that both of you are hysterical?" Addison raised an eyebrow.

Marren laughed, "Drunk stories from last weekend. Toilet paper stuck on shoes; break ups in the middle of the dance floor. You know, drunk bar life."

"Ophelia told me to let you both know she's running a little late but will be here soon. She had a late client meeting." Seth smiled, giving the women his wife's message.

"Sounds good. I'm on a mission to get tipsy and flirt my ass off with some cute boys." Addison laughed while wiggling her eyebrows.

Brogan stepped up, taking the seat on the opposite side of Marren. His smile was wide as he said, "I hope I can be included in that mission."

"Hey Brogan, I always flirt with you; that's just a given." Addison winked at him.

"I want to introduce you to my business partner and friend Max Ross." Brogan looked at Max then at the women introducing them, "this is Marren Quinn and Addison Jacobs."

Max had yet to take a seat. Stepping forward, he extended his hand to Marren first, then reached over to shake Addison's. His eyes smiled when he spoke, "It's nice to meet you both. I've heard some fun stories."

Marren snickered, "I bet. We didn't think you existed, the mysterious business partner." Marren quoted in the air with her fingers when she said business partner.

Brogan laughed, "I'm warning you Max, these girls are tough."

Max nodded with a smirk, "Noted."

Seth placed a beer in front of Brogan. "What can I get you Max?" Seth held out his hand, "I'm Seth by the way, Ophelia's husband."

"I knew that, have heard good things. Your wife is a brilliant lawyer. Brogan and I have the upmost respect for her. She's made our business dealings a breeze."

Seth was full of pride at hearing his wife's praises, "Good to hear. She's amazing if I do say so myself." Seth smiled with a knowing nod.

"I'll take a beer. IPA?" Max asked.

"You got it."

Max shifted his body, returning his attention to Brogan who was talking with the ladies.

"Addison, what's going on with you? You've been busy with work and missing our mid-week drinking," Brogan asked.

"I know. Work has been a little crazy. I have a case that's taking up most of my time. Not great timing since the weather is so amazing. Can us girls take you up on your offer to hang out at the pool and lazy river at the country club?"

Brogan confirmed, "You know you can. Let me know when and I'll get you the passes and what you need." Brogan took a drink of his beer.

"Thank you. How did it go with the pretty brunette last weekend?" Addison inquired, raising an eyebrow.

"She was pretty and twenty five years old. We didn't have much in common." Brogan offered a disappointed smile, "I need to be able to talk about something other than college life and drink specials, and she was too young."

"Well you don't look like a twenty five year old woman is too young for you, that's why that age group hits on you," Addison offered a sweet smile and a touch of her hand to Brogan's forearm.

"Such a charmer tonight, I think the flirting is going to be severe for some lucky guy."

Addison giggled, "I'm being serious. It's just our curse, we look young."

Brogan leaned his beer to hers and gave her a clink in agreement.

The pairs broke off into conversations with Addison and Marren turning towards each other and Brogan listening to Max. When Marren turned to talk with Addison she received a wide-eyed smile.

"Oh God, I know what that look is for. Yes, he is exactly your type. Holy Shit hot," Marren laughed.

Addison's girly giggle took hold. She covered her mouth and spoke quietly, "He's kind of dreamy. Like 'easy to get undressed for' dreamy."

Max Ross stood six foot two inches tall, with a chiseled build. His hair was dark and styled in a very GQ way, not too short, not too long with a little sculpted lift at the top, just enough to run your fingers through. His eyes were green and he smiled easily with beautiful white teeth. The goatee that surrounded his mouth was well trimmed and sexy. He wore khaki cargo shorts, flip-flops and a button down dress shirt with the sleeves rolled to the elbows.

Marren laughed out loud, "Where did you come up with that?"

"I don't know? I don't think I've seen that hot of a boy in a while." Addison smiled, turning slightly towards Brogan, then she looked back at Marren, "they are speaking Spanish."

"How well do you know the blonde?" Max asked Brogan, speaking in Spanish.

Brogan responded in Spanish, "FBI, one of Ophelia's friends. Smart, funny, obviously a looker. She's in her early thirties I believe. Not sure she's dating anyone now but I don't think it's serious if she is."

Again Max kept up the Spanish, "She's beautiful, sexy, I would really enjoy her body; wouldn't mind taking her home." Max took a sip of his beer.

Brogan chuckled and replied in Spanish, "Maybe you should talk to her first. You should have come out for a beer when I asked you months ago."

Max rolled his eyes giving Brogan a smart-ass look. In Spanish he replied with a chuckle, "Very funny, I know to talk to a woman before asking them to come home with me. You know I've been working; distractions are not an option right now. She looks like more distraction than I can handle."

Their conversation continued in Spanish, but the subject changed to work related topics.

Ophelia walked in and said hello to everyone before ushering the group to move to the back patio where tables were pulled together for their group. She listened to Max and Brogan finish their conversation in Spanish while she walked with everyone to the patio.

"Your Spanish is getting better Brogan," Ophelia complimented.

"Thank you. I've been trying to talk to Max in Spanish as much as possible. It's working."

Ophelia nodded offering, "You know Addison speaks fluent

Spanish, she would be another person you could practice with."

Addison looked at Max and Brogan with a wide smile before pursing her lips together.

Brogan laughed, "I didn't know that. Isn't that something?" He gave Max a pat on the shoulder.

Max, embarrassed and uncomfortable, gave Addison an apologetic look.

Addison leaned into Max with a flirty smile, "I hope you talk to me first." She wanted to make sure Max knew she heard every word he said. The corners of Max's mouth turned up, giving her a sexy grin. Addison felt her heart skip.

The women sat across the table from the men. Max had a perfect view of Addison, who was trying not to look at him but failed miserably enough times that he noticed her attention. Luckily, eligible bachelors approached Addison, Marren and Ophelia to flirt and talk, distracting her from Max.

Brogan nudged Max, "You better make a move. Addison's dance card usually fills up."

Seth laughed, "She's picky, she might dance with them but she has a criteria they have to meet to sit at the table. I wouldn't worry too much about the guys, I'd worry about the criteria."

Seth and Brogan laughed.

"I'm charming. You don't think I'll meet the criteria? How picky is she?" Max took a drink of his beer.

Seth gave Max's shoulder a manly clap, "Step up to the plate and take your chances. Looks like that one was just shot down."

The three men looked at some young guy walking away.

Addison turned catching their eyes. She smiled, "What?"

"What was wrong with that one?" Seth asked.

Addison shrugged, "Too young and the last concert he went to was Justin Beiber." Addison took a drink of her beer.

Marren and Ophelia laughed, and Ophelia asked, "When did you start asking that question?"

"Hey, that question says a lot about a person," Addison smirked, taking another drink of her beer.

Max smiled at Addison asking, "Who did you see in concert last?"

"I went to Hang Out Fest in Gulf Shores. Several bands but my favorite was Anderson East. He's kind of bluesy and put on a good show."

Marren nodded in agreement, "Yep, I agree. He has a sexy voice."

Addison looked at Max, "And you?"

The men held their breath. This was it, either Max would continue to talk to Addison, or this is where it would all end.

"I took a date to see Ed Sheeran for her birthday, when he was in Tampa."

Addison nodded with a soft smile, "Sounds like she had a good birthday." She held a good poker face, not letting any of the men know if Max made the cut.

The night went on with good conversation and laughter. When Marren was asked to dance and left the table, Max made his way around to stand next to Addison.

"So I'm at a major disadvantage," Max said with flirty confidence.

Addison looked up at him, "How so?"

"You heard what I said about you when I was talking to Brogan. But I don't know if I passed the concert test." Max took a drink of his beer.

Addison tried not to smile, "Did you want to pass the test?"

Max didn't answer, instead the corners of his mouth curled up. "Tell me something about you."

"What do you want to know? Better yet, tell me what you think you know about me. You've been watching me all night," Addison flirted.

Max gave her a sideways smile, leaning in to talk in her ear, "Ok. Let's see, you don't let the men that come to talk to you buy you a beer because you don't want them to think they have the right to stick around." Max pulled back to look in her eyes where he found confirmation. He continued, "you would rather sit and talk with your friends than spend time with a man you're not interested in." Addison smirked and nodded. "You find me attractive and want to dance with me." Max's eyes danced with flirtation.

"You think so, huh?" Addison took a drink of her beer.

Max put his beer down, taking Addison's hand, "Will you dance with me?"

Addison bit the corner of her lower lip, "Yes." She placed her beer on the high top table.

Max had waited for the band to play something slow so he could pull her body close to his. Walking her to the center of the dance floor, he turned, taking her in his arms.

Max held Addison's waist tight with one hand, and her hand in the other. His breath was on her neck when he complimented her, "You're gorgeous."

"Thank you. You're not so bad yourself." She smiled and let her hand run up his thick bicep to his shoulder. "So you're the chef Brogan brags about."

Max smiled, "He brags about me?" He pulled his face back to look at her, raising an inquisitive eyebrow.

"I hear you're an amazing chef." Addison stated.

Max gave a small nod, "I hear that on occasion."

"Modest too." Addison rolled her eyes.

Max turned his head, touching his cheek to her forehead, "You smell good." Her shampoo and perfume were intoxicating.

Addison's face was in the nape of Max's neck, "So do you."

When the song ended, Max continued to hold her. Not wanting his time with her to end he asked, "Can I buy you a beer? Sit next to you and talk?"

Addison smiled, "I would like that."

Max's hand held Addison's lower back as they returned to the table to join their friends. This time Max sat next to Addison. They had several beers and enjoyed talking with not only each other but their friends as well. The two danced every slow song, giving Max an opportunity to hold Addison close. With every hour that went by, friends started leaving one by one. By two o'clock in the morning, Max and Addison were the only two left sitting at the bar with just sips left in their beer bottles.

"We've closed the place. I guess we should get out of here so the staff can go home," Addison acknowledged, watching the employees cleaning up the night's festivities.

Max nodded and stood with Addison. He couldn't help but place his hand on the small of her back while walking out the front door. While sitting together, a portion of their bodies were constantly touching, thigh-to-thigh, hip-to-hip or occasionally he brushed her hair from her face with his fingers. Each time he touched her he felt a charge that only made him want to touch her more.

"Where did you park?"

"Right here," Addison stood in front of her golf cart. "I only live a few blocks from the bar." She hitched her thumb in the direction she would be taking home.

Max closed the distance between them, lacing his fingers through her hair. His voice was rough when he spoke, "I'm going to kiss you Addison."

His lips brushed hers gently with his tongue tracing her bottom lip. "I'm not ready to say goodnight. Are you?" His lips kissed her mouth thoroughly, his tongue caressing the seam of her mouth, and his hands holding the nape of her neck, tilting her head back to have her mouth the way he wanted before he took the kiss deeper. Addison's lips parted, inviting his tongue to tangle with hers.

Addison's fingers wrinkled his shirt, tightening her grip at his waist. His kiss made her head fuzzy, lighting her on fire; she didn't want the night to end.

When Max broke the kiss with soft lips raking over hers she stammered, "Do you want to?" Addison eyes looked towards the golf cart.

"Yes, I do."

Max was eager to get her home. Walking to the driver's side of the golf cart, Addison lowered herself to the seat and slid over, letting Max drive. Addison fidgeted, holding the handle of the cart with white knuckles while Max drove at top speed, which wasn't as fast as he would have liked, but as fast as the golf cart would go. He drove with care, but Addison looked nervous. He figured it was from what they would be doing once they reached their destination and not the ride. Without stating the obvious, he knew why Addison started talking about landscaping, it wasn't the norm for her to bring a man home for a one-night stand and she needed to occupy her mind with something other than how she planned to finish her night out. Addison pointed out several houses that had well manicured lawns and pretty coach lights, she explained she bought her house three months prior and had focused on the inside and had yet to spend time getting the front and backyard the way she wanted. Max smiled and listened to the landscape ideas while receiving directions to her house.

"Do you know why they call it the Fruit and Nut District?" Addison blushed, "Street names. I live on Walnut." She realized she had not stopped talking the entire ride to her home. Closing her mouth for a few moments and giving his ears a break, she once again spoke up. "This is me." She pointed to her driveway and took the garage door opener out of the glove compartment, pushing the button.

Max pulled the golf cart in and parked while Addison used the remote to close the garage door. She hopped out of the cart quickly with Max following her to the door. She opened the door and entered with Max walking in behind her. They entered from the garage into a beautiful kitchen.

Addison smiled shyly asking, "Would you like something to drink?"

"Water sounds good."

Addison retrieved two bottles of water from the refrigerator, handing one to Max.

She sighed, "I'm sorry. I know I was talking your ear off. I'm nervous. I don't, I haven't…"

Max interrupted Addison by taking her hand and placing it on his chest. She could feel his heart pounding. "I'm nervous too. Show me around your new house."

Addison started the tour. "My favorite part of the kitchen is the island. I use it for about everything. I eat here, use my computer here, I really like the open floor plan and this is kind of the center gathering place."

She continued the tour, showing him the dining room and living room. They walked to the back of the house.

"I don't use the dining room but you never know. There are three sets of French doors, dining room, living room and off the master bedroom that exit to the back yard." They both looked out the living room doors to the backyard. "I want the patio to extend the length of the house in the backyard. That's not done yet."

She walked towards the front door to the small hallway on the left. Max followed.

"Spare bedroom that faces the front of the house, bathroom, second spare bedroom I changed to an office, and that's the Master bedroom." Addison pointed. "The Master has a bathroom as well. I'll show you my favorite thing about the house."

She walked through the master bedroom and into the bathroom.

"This tub sold me," Addison giggled. They stood in front of a vintage claw foot bathtub. She added with a little moan, "It's amazing."

Max smiled, thinking of Addison soaking in the tub. She was right, that would be amazing.

"Your face lights up when you talk about the house. This was meant for you; it's beautiful," Max complimented.

Addison smiled, "Thank you. I think it was meant for me too."

She turned and walked into the Master bedroom. Suddenly, he took her hand. He placed his water bottle on the dresser to his left and took her water bottle, putting it next to his.

Max wrapped his arms around her. Kissing her cheek and neck, he asked, "Still nervous?"

"Not so much."

Addison's mouth met his, surrendering her lips and tongue for the taking. Max held the nape of her neck and with his other arm wrapped around her, he guided them to the edge of her bed. Addison's hands pushed under his shirt, touching then holding tightly to his lower back. Max's body was warm and muscular to the touch. He found the zipper to her sundress between her shoulder blades and unzipped it to her lower back. When his fingers ran over her back, he felt Addison take a deep breath and press her fingers into his back, holding him tighter. He pulled the spaghetti straps down her shoulders and the dress fell to her feet. Max wrapped her up in a tight hug before releasing her so Addison could step out of the dress. Max picked up the floral dress and placed it over the footboard of the bed. His eyes raked over her body. Addison stood before him in a black strapless bra and black lacy bikini panties.

Max's voice sounded gruff with need, "My God you are beautiful."

Addison smiled, "You need to catch up."

She reached for the buttons of his dress shirt. She started at the top and he helped with a few at the bottom. Addison slid the shirt off of his shoulders for Max to finish removing it. He placed it with her dress.

Her hands ran over his chest and abdomen, feeling his muscles contract. Addison swallowed hard and wrapping her arms around his neck, she pressed her body to his, taking her lips to his mouth. Her kiss was passionate, exploring his mouth and tongue. Max had wrapped her up in his arms for a moment but let go to remove his cargo shorts. Once the shorts were bunched at his feet, he gathered her in his arms again. His fingers trailed up her back, finding the clasp of her bra. He unfastened it, slipping the bra from between them.

Max's hands ran down her back, up her sides, into her hair and finally his arms circled her, lifting her off of her feet to place her in the middle of her bed. His body partially covered her with his leg between her legs. Max kissed her mouth and neck, caressed her breast and excited her nipple with his thumb. His mouth continued to roam her neck to her collarbone and shoulder. Her breasts were kissed gently and explored, but only after every inch was worshipped did he concentrate on her nipples. His tongue flicked and his teeth teased until he drew the pretty pink flesh into his mouth, contracting his lips creating a vacuum. Addison's head turned gently side-to-side as she whimpered soft sounds. Her fingers on her left hand laced through his hair while her other hand held his shoulder. Max paid close attention to Addison's breathing and the noises she made to ensure she was enjoying every touch. Spending the same time and attention on both breasts had Addison squirming beneath him. His mouth moved up while his hand moved down, gently running over her stomach to the edge of her panties. Max kissed Addison's mouth gently and he lifted his head to look at her.

He used the name her friends called her when he asked, "Addie, any second thoughts?"

Addison looked at him, knowing he could see how desperate she was to have him. "No," she whispered.

Max covered her mouth with his, giving her gentle, open mouthed kisses. His hand slipped under the lace of her underwear, finding her warm and turned on. His fingers explored, finding the spot that made Addison's body arch towards him. He circled his index finger, running it up and down the spot that was setting her on fire. Addison's head turned away from him, her moans were soft and breathy.

Max kissed her neck, "You are so ready for me. Is that what you want?" Max slid two fingers inside her, lifting his face to watch her body respond. Addison arched her neck and moaned with pleasure.

He continued to move his fingers, crooking them towards her inner wall, moving them gently in and out as he watched her.

Addison's fingers clinched his forearm. Her teeth raked her bottom lip and she lazily blinked, meeting his gaze.

He brushed her lips with his lips, "Is this good?" He picked up a little speed.

Addison's eyes rolled and she closed her lids, "Yes," she panted.

Max continued with his fingers, adding his thumb to circle her on the outside. He heard her exhale and a sexy moan escaped.

He whispered in her ear, "I want you to come. I want to make you feel good. Let me have it, Addie."

Addison was almost out of her mind. She was moments from losing herself. She held tight to his forearm and her other hand clenched the blankets on the bed. Her body quaked and the tingle took over, shooting from her center to curl her toes.

"Oh My God," came from her lips in a breathy groan. She felt her body spasm and tighten around Max's fingers. Max soothed her with gentle kisses while she rode out the quake of her orgasm. Before she was back down to earth, Addison wrapped her arms around Max and pulled him to cover her body. Needy and hot, she said, "I want you inside me."

Max kissed her deep then pushed away, removing his boxer briefs and retrieving a condom from his cargo shorts. He rolled it on and touched her sweetly, removing her panties. Max found his place between her legs. Lowering himself to her, he held the nape of her neck, giving her mouth gentle kisses. He held his body up slightly with his arm extended on the bed while he slowly pushed, entering her with the tip of his cock.

Addison's eyes met his. She blinked slowly.

He kissed her with the softest kiss she had ever received, "I'll go slow." Max was large and beyond turned on. The fit was tight, but her body began to relax, adjusting to his size. He eased his way in, briefly pulling out slightly then pushing back in, giving her body time to enjoy him before moving deep. He continued moving in and out, adding depth with every push. Both of her hands planted on the cheeks of his ass not to force him in deeper, just so she could feel the thrust. Addison's head lifted off the bed, her mouth seeking his. Max lowered his lips to hers. Releasing the nape of her neck, his hand cupped her breast, touching and caressing.

"You feel so good." Max's voice was strained. He had thrust in fully, feeling her body take him in completely. His hand moved back to her neck with his thumb caressing her cheek, "You are so sexy, so beautiful. Jesus, Addie, I'm not going to last. You have to come for me."

Max picked up the pace; his hand reached down and pushed her knee up slightly to get just a little deeper.

Addison's voice was breathy as she whimpered, "I'm there, Oh God I'm there."

Her body clenched, heaved and she clung to him tight as the waves of pleasure went through her. Max continued his climb for a few more moments until he exhaled hard and his sexy, manly groan was buried in her hair.

Addison's eyes closed, holding tight to Max's body that felt heavy and wonderful on top of her. She knew she was in trouble with this man, not wanting this to be just one night. Max rolled his body to her side, pulling her to rest her head on his chest. Addison's cheek felt the hard beat of his heart begin to slow and his breathing begin to return to normal. Her body tingled even still and his fingers running up and down her back didn't ease the fire, they only kept it going.

Max kissed her forehead, "I'll be right back."

When he returned from the bathroom, Addison was standing, waiting to take her turn. Max sat on the edge of the bed waiting. When she opened the bathroom door he smiled and motioned to her with his head to come to him. Addison smiled coyly and sauntered over. He reached out and snatched her, pulling her to stand between his legs. Addison giggled, holding on to his shoulders while he ran his mouth and face along the crook of her neck.

Max smiled at her laughter, "I think I can do even better; let's try this again." Before Addison could speak she was on her back, receiving kisses and caresses.

"I wasn't complaining, it was…" Addison's breath caught and her head turned to the side.

Max's mouth enveloped her nipple suckling hard, and his hand cupped the other breast, preparing it for his mouth.

"What was it?" Max asked before giving her other nipple attention.

"Mmmm," Addison's soft voice responded to his tongue on her.

Her chest heaved a deep breath and his fingers ran down her stomach, feeling the contraction. "Your skin is so soft, so touchable," he hummed.

His mouth opened, covering her lips with a caressing kiss as he ran the back of his fingers up her inner thigh, feeling goose bumps form before making their way to his destination. His fingers stroked between her legs. Hearing the little moan come from Addison's throat into their kiss, he continued working his fingers. Addison couldn't continue to kiss him, her head fell to the side and she nibbled at her lip, her breathing was fast.

Max slowed his touch, "I want your mouth."

Addison waited a moment and turned her face to him, "You're making me crazy."

Max raked his teeth across her bottom lip, his tongue teased and flirted with hers and his hand left her body, finding her hand.

Placing her hand on his erection he said, "Feel what you do to me."

Addison stroked, feeling the solid length of him. Max's fingers returned to her, two slipping inside with a bend, honing in on her G spot.

"You are so ready for me Addie. I want to be inside you again."

"Yes." Addison arched her back, lifting towards him. "Oh God, Yes," she panted in a sexy, jagged voice that sounded as if she was suffering without him.

"Do you have condoms?" Max had only brought one, not prepared for meeting Addison.

"Medicine cabinet," she stated.

Max kissed her, "Don't move." He stepped away.

He opened the medicine cabinet finding an unopened box of condoms sitting next to a foiled rectangle of monthly birth control pills. He opened them, seeing that the prescription was current and being taken. Addison's knees were bent and touching each other, with her feet on the bed when Max returned with the condom. He kissed her knees, opening them, placing one on either side of his body. His mouth continued to climb and raking his facial hair across her stomach, he felt her squirm.

"A little ticklish?" he asked with a grin. His lips continued to climb, grazing over both nipples; he felt Addison's fingers weave through his hair.

Max's mouth touched hers in a gentle kiss before he pulled back to look at her and ask, "How long have you been on the pill?"

Addison's eyes met his, "Couple years."

He nodded, "I get all the check ups I'm supposed to, clean bill of health. You?"

She nodded.

Max gave her a chaste kiss. "I can still wear the condom if you want me to but I would love to feel just you. Should I wrap it?"

Addison shook her head no with one turn and found his lips. Her kiss was demanding and forceful. Her tongue found his and her lips moved to all corners of his mouth.

Max exhaled a soft noise and grabbed on to her hips. He pushed up, standing at the side of the bed and pulling Addison's body to the edge. Max held her knees in the palms of his hands, her feet planted on the edge of the mattress. The tip of him tickled to enter her.

Addison's eyes were on his as he gently thrust about half way in and pulled out slightly. Max thrust a little deeper and circled his hips. Addison's body arched and she moaned. Her head turned to the side and her eyes shut. Max's hands moved from her knees to the top of her hips where her back came off the bed in the inviting arch. Max pulled her to him as he pushed into her, going deeper and deeper with every thrust. His pace was steady as he watched her on the brink of coming undone.

"Christ, you are so sexy." Max was winded, "I want you to come."

Addison gave a melodious breathy, "Harder."

Max's plunge was deep and hard, causing a smacking noise against her body. His pace rapid and lustful, giving her all of him in a forceful thrust over and over until her body clenched around his. The waves of orgasm from Addison pulsed, tightening around him. He watched her mouth moan his name before he bent forward placing his lips on hers. His kiss invaded her mouth, demanding and electric.

"Roll over Addison," his voice was gruff.

Max backed up, letting Addison position herself to be taken from behind. He pulled her body back to put her on her feet in front of him, she bent forward over the edge of the bed and he lifted one of her knees, placing it on the mattress.

Max eased in, "Is this ok?"

"Mmmm hmmm," Addison replied.

Max pounded into her, feeling her contract around him. His fingers held her hair at the scalp, giving a soft tug as his other hand reached around to stroke between her legs. Addison shook and quaked.

"Max, I'm… Oh God." Her voice was breathy and low-pitched.

"You feel so fucking good. I'm right behind you."

Max's orgasm was fierce, pulsing through him. He kissed her shoulder, raking his teeth for a slight nip. His arms held tight to her body, keeping her in place while he filled her.

Sweaty and spent, they both collapsed gently on the bed. Addison turned away from him, lying facedown on the bed. Max's body partially covered hers with his arm wrapped around her middle. They were both exhausted and in awe of each other.

CHAPTER 2

"So how did you guys leave it?" Ophelia asked, taking a bite of her quiche from R Bistro. She and Addison met for lunch at the restaurant on Fairhope Avenue.

Addison took a sip of tea, "Leave what? It was nice to meet him."

Ophelia laughed, "Really, you are full of shit if you think you are getting off that easy. You were both enjoying yourselves at the bar. Is that where it ended?"

"I'm not going to talk about it. It was just one off those things. He was fun." Addison raised an eyebrow; "I have a date this Saturday with the bartender from here. He's cute right?"

Ophelia glanced at the bartender, "Very cute. What about Max?"

Addison shrugged, "I told you what he said to Brogan, he wasn't looking for any distractions. I'm not looking for something casual. He just happened, it was a fluke, nothing more. Call it lonely, call it poor judgment or finding him drop dead gorgeous and irresistible that night, whatever – it's nothing and not going to happen again."

Ophelia smirked and sat back, "You convincing me or yourself?"

Addison laughed, "It's Thursday, he hasn't called." She shrugged.

"You didn't exchange phone numbers," Ophelia clarified.

"Right, but Brogan has my number. So it would be easy enough to get my number if he wanted it. He's not at all what I'm looking for."

"I think you should call her. What's so demanding that you can't date the girl? It's obvious that you are interested in Addison; you've brought her up several times this week." Brogan sat back in the barstool watching the staff scurrying around and getting ready for the Saturday night dinner rush.

"I haven't brought her up. You have. I don't have the time to spend on a relationship and that girl is not casual. She's anything but. Stop pushing." Max walked behind the bar, retrieving the wine he planned to cook with.

Brogan laughed, "I am not the one who brought her up. You just asked if I've seen her this week, which means you are inquiring."

"No, I was just curious. You all get together often, that's all it was." Max shook his head, "I need to get back to the kitchen. I'll see you tomorrow."

"Hey Addison, how are you?" Brogan asked, approaching her and what looked like her date.

Addison looked up surprised, "Hi Brogan. I'm good. How about you?"

"Good." Brogan looked at the man sitting next to her, "Scott, right?"

"Yes. Nice to see you again." Scott shook Brogan's hand. "Have you found a better lunch hang out?"

Brogan laughed, "I've been in Orange Beach at lunch time lately. R Bistro is my favorite gumbo in town. I'll be in soon. How's are you doing flipping houses?"

Scott smiled, happy that Brogan remembered their conversations. "Really well. I have two for sale right now. Just purchased another Bay House on County Road 1."

"Good for you. It was nice to see you." Brogan looked at Addison, "Beers and a Burger on Wednesday after yoga?"

"That's the only reason I go to yoga," she laughed.

Brogan kissed her on the cheek, "See you soon. Have fun."

Brogan smiled, catching the eye of the new female friend he was meeting. He met her at the door and sat by the window. During drinks with his friend he sent Max a text message.

Brogan: Ran in to Addison. She's on a date. Maybe you should re-think your stance on calling her?

Max: Addison is free to do anything she wants. Thanks for the info. Get back to your own love life.

Max could feel his face flush. He was not happy. It had been a week since the fireworks they both felt and she was already dating. Max shook his head and reminded himself that had no right to have an opinion about anything she did. He wasn't getting involved, that's why he didn't ask for her phone number or give her his number. It was an amazing one-time thing. Max's plans were to open the franchises and his own restaurant; no woman was getting in the way of that.

Two weeks later, Addison was on another dinner date with Scott at Bone and Barrel Restaurant and Bar. They sat along the wall at a two top and were in a fun conversation about Scott's business when she noticed Brogan and Max walk in and take a seat at the bar. Addison didn't make eye contact with either of the men and continued giving her full attention to Scott. They both finished their meal and polished off an additional beer before making their way to the front doors, taking their leave. It was nearly 8:30pm and Scott knew Addison had plans with Marren and Ophelia at 9:30pm but convinced her to meet him for dinner beforehand. Scott kissed her cheek and hugged her saying he would see her soon before they walked separate ways down Fairhope Avenue. Addison was meeting Ophelia at the Fly Bar and from the text she just received, Ophelia was waiting.

Marren walked in Bone and Barrel taking a seat at the bar. She asked, "Hey Seth, have you seen Addie and Ophelia? I'm meeting them and ran late?"

"Addison just left a few minutes ago, I'm expecting both of them back here." Seth was behind the bar making drinks.

Marren looked at her phone, "Never mind, they are at Fly Bar."

Seth looked at her and raised an eyebrow. "My wife is pissed at me so she's cheating on the bar." He shook his head, "I'll walk down with you and make up with her so she comes and sits in our bar." He chuckled.

Brogan and Max laughed, listening to Seth.

"What's she pissed at you about?" Brogan inquired.

"I told her she has to hire a paralegal to do some of the work at her practice. She's pregnant and tired. She needs some help. She's a redhead and stubborn as all get out. Let me go do a little makin' up."

Seth had another bartender take over and walked to the Fly Bar with Marren, it was just around the corner, not even a five-minute walk.

Addison and Ophelia were sitting at the bar talking with Amy the bartender.

Seth smiled, "Hey Amy, How are you?"

"Good. You?"

"Very good." Seth smiled then turned his attention to his wife. He looked at Ophelia with a half smile, "How is my beautiful wife?"

"Mad at you," she scoffed.

Seth wrapped his arms around her, "I see that." Seth nuzzled his face in her neck, "I love you more than anything. I want you happy and rested so we can enjoy your pregnancy. You are going to do this for me. I need you to." He kissed her neck.

Ophelia sighed, "I love you. I will."

Seth smiled kissing her lips, "Promise? Next week you hire someone?"

"I promise."

Seth touched her face and whispered, "There's going to be some good makin' up lovin' tonight." He put a kiss on her that made her swoon.

Ophelia laughed, "Go back to work."

Seth laughed, "Have fun. Come visit your lonely husband behind the bar."

Addison smiled, "Told you. He's not bossing you. He just wants you to get some rest."

Ophelia sighed, "My hormones are crazy. He's right, but I'm a control freak and hate the idea of turning things over to someone else."

Marren smiled, "You are managing the people you hire. Let them do the work and check it over before it goes anywhere. It's a good move. You can't grow and take on more clients if you are tied up doing every detail."

The women finished their drinks and walked over to Bone and Barrel, taking their place at the bar. Addison chose the seat furthest away from Max, sitting next to Marren.

It wasn't long before Max walked over to stand next to Addison, "How have you been?"

"Good, thank you. How have you been?"

Max acknowledged her cool and incredibly polite tone. "Good. Working. The restaurant has been busy. Can I get you another beer?"

"No thank you. I'm good for now. That's good to hear about the restaurant. Brogan was saying on Wednesday that you have a couple franchises opening in the next few months."

Max nodded, "We do and with inquiries for a few more. How has work been for you?"

"Fine. I'm working a case that has many moving parts. I'm getting a ton of reports and paperwork dumped on my desk. Should keep me busy." Addison was ready for him to go away; enough of the small talk. She was uncomfortable and he smelled so damn good. Addison took a drink of her beer.

"How was your date?" Max turned, leaning his back against the bar in a smug stance.

"It was nice." Addison looked forward, not meeting his eyes.

He watched her, "It ended early."

"My date is none of your business. But for your information, he wanted to have dinner and knew I was meeting the girls at 9:30pm." Addison was not rude, just abrupt.

"Nice guy?" Max raised an eyebrow.

"Yes, of course. What's with the questions?"

"Just curious."

"Well, be curious about something other than my love life." Addison gave a curt smile.

Max smiled, "I'm getting the impression you might not be very happy with me."

Addison shook her head, "I'm fine. Indifferent really. I just don't like to kiss and tell. Maybe choose a different subject to talk about."

"I didn't see you kiss him so what would there be to tell?" Max smirked.

Addison blushed, "I'm trying to figure out why you are over here talking to me. After all I'm a distraction right?"

Max nodded, putting his hand on his chest, "I'm wounded. You don't want my company?" Max grinned, not letting her answer, "You've distracted me for two weeks. I've thought about you many times. I should have called."

Addie answered, "You were fun but not what I'm looking for. I want someone that would go the extra mile to see me again. You're not that guy."

"Ok. I get that. That doesn't mean we can't be friends. Let me buy you dinner at my restaurant, come in and I'll cook for you."

"Friends?" Addison laughed, "You want to be friends?"

"Absolutely. You're smart, fun, an amazing conversationalist," Max raised an eyebrow, teasing her. "We have mutual friends and I am a nice guy. What do you say? Give me a chance. I can be a good friend."

Addison shrugged, "Maybe."

She could tell by the way he was looking her up and down that he could never be just her friend. But dinner sounded inviting.

"Maybe." He nodded, "I work all day Sunday. If you're in the area, I'll feed you."

"Thank you for the invitation." Addison smiled, taking a sip of her beer. She excused herself to use the restroom and when she returned, Max had taken his seat back next to Brogan. She managed to avoid making eye contact with him for the rest of the evening.

Additional Books by Ansley Prescott

Lean more:

www.ansleyprescott.com

Forever Fairhope Series:

Fairhope Ophelia

Fairhope Addison (Coming September 2019)

Fairhope Paisley (Coming October 2019)

Fairhope Jubileigh (Coming November 2019)

Fairhope Marren (Coming December 2019)

Fairhope Magnolia (Coming 2020)

Fairhope Delilah (Coming 2020)

Stand Alone Romance Books

Friends with Benefits